MW01130374

ALL WORKS BY
BENJAMIN WALLACE

DUCK & COVER ADVENTURES
Post-Apocalyptic Nomadic Warriors (A Duck & Cover Adventure Book 1)
Knights of the Apocalypse (A Duck & Cover Adventure Book 2)
Last Band of the Apocalypse: A Duck & Cover Adventurette
Prisoner's Dilemma: A Duck & Cover Adventurette
How to Host an Intervention: A Duck & Cover Prequel
Gone to the Dogs: A Duck & Cover Prequel

BULLETPROOF ADVENTURES OF DAMIAN STOCKWELL
Horror in Honduras (The Bulletproof Adventures of Damian Stockwell)
Terrors of Tesla (The Bulletproof Adventures of Damian Stockwell)
The Mechanical Menace (The Bulletproof Adventures of Damian Stockwell)

DAD VERSUS
Dad Versus The Grocery Store
Dad Versus Halloween
Dad Versus Santa
Dad Versus The Tooth Fairy
Dad Versus Democracy
Dads Versus The World (Volume 1)
Dads Versus Zombies

OTHER BOOKS
Tortugas Rising

UNCIVIL
UnCivil: The Immortal Engine
UnCivil: Vanderbilt's Behemoth

SHORT STORIES
Alternate Realty
Dystopia Inc. #1: The War Room
Pilgrim (A Short Story)

Visit benjaminwallacebooks.com for more info.

By

Benjamin Wallace

ISBN-13: 978-1479199440
ISBN-10: 1479199443

Cover design by J. Caleb Design.

Dedicated to my wife.
Because she's hot.

1

An island paradise was no place to die, but every hand-selected vine that tripped up his feet and each branch that slapped him wet across the face slowed his escape and brought this possible end ever closer.

Lush vegetation, imported and landscaped in every detail to mimic a rainforest, choked the light from the day deep within its thickest growth. Shafts of light cast from the noon sun broke meekly through the canopy, casting shadow and confusion before anyone who chose to stroll beneath its magnificence and masking danger for those forced to move at a faster pace.

This was where he ran.

Sweat broke from his face with every step, and threatened his vision as salt from his brow stung at his eyes; every rushed step was a danger. Broad strokes of his arms swiped the perspiration away as he listened for more than the sound of his own heavy breathing.

There was nothing.

They had been right behind him, so close that their steps threatened to stomp the shoes from his heels only moments before. He prayed that his hastily beaten path through the thick growth had lost them. But he knew that he was outnumbered and lost.

Escape was close in any direction. White sand and surf surrounded the island, and any shore would lead to his salvation, but in his escape he had unknowingly charged toward the island's center, taking him ever further from freedom.

Going back was not an option. He pushed further in. The entire cay was only twenty acres, but the dense foliage tripled the distance that he had to walk. Vines snared his feet as he stumbled through the simulated rainforest. He cursed the owner that had made such a realistic recreation possible.

The crash of vegetation sounded behind him, stalks of thick plants cried out as they were snapped. His dash had not thrown off his pursuers; broken boughs and leaves had made tracking him easy.

Charging forward, head down and hands out, had bought him some time and won him countless scratches from thorn bushes. He bled in a hundred places; his black clothes were torn ragged and hung like drapes from the collar around his neck. He dove farther into the rainforest and realized he was more lost than he had intended to be. His sense of direction was turned on end by the meandering path that he had forced into the jungle's floor as he stepped broadly over the ground cover, ducked under branches, and danced around the trunks of trees.

Sand wasn't far in any direction. Eventually he would emerge on a beach, head north and get to safety.

Voices. Shouts. They gained on him. Every sound gave them away. It was an advantage he could do nothing to exploit. He held a pistol tight within his hand, but he knew from the weight that there were few rounds left in the weapon. Still, he waved it at the sounds that seem to surround him.

Constant clicks emitted from the black box in his other hand. This rhythmic beat matched his pulse; it was constant, quick and strong.

He held still, ears sharp, listening for another splintered stalk. But all was quiet again, except for the box in his hand. His predators were silent once more.

Mud flew from his heels as he raced and kicked the grip of thorns from his pants and shoes. Then there was another noise. The roar of rushing water broke through the dense growth. Convinced it was the crash of surf, he rushed toward the sound and found himself moving up a steep incline. The sound became all but deafening; the roar swallowed the ambient sounds of the man-made jungle. He broke through the vegetation and into unfiltered daylight.

It was not the shoreline. It was a river's edge.

He peered over a twenty-foot gorge and saw that a river tore through the island's center. Powerful pumps that drove the current added a mechanical pulse to the river's constant thrum.

"You've got to be kidding." He paced the bank looking for a bridge or catwalk. There was no way to cross.

A quick look upstream and down led him to believe that whichever multi-millionaire had ordered the island enjoyed white water rafting. It was hardly a peaceful stream. White crested waves tore the waterway apart to generate a challenging run for the weekend kayaker.

Boulders lined the edges and rose from the riverbed. Whether they were real or fake, he couldn't tell. He set the black box down. It continued to click.

A trained move of his thumb dropped the magazine from the pistol into his hand. Two rounds sat atop the spring-loaded driver. Three total. Several hunters stalked him. Even luck couldn't hit all of them with just three bullets.

He jammed the mag back into the grip and looked back into the rapids. His science teacher's voice echoed in his head: "all rivers eventually lead to the ocean."

Sound advice in a natural world but, Mr. Stiegelmeyer could never have imagined this. This river could lead to the ocean. Or it could lead to a series of pumps. There was no way to tell.

He studied the waves as they bounced off the rocks. Reading the water was difficult. The artificial waterway could be as shallow as a couple of feet or run all the way to the ocean's floor.

The river was designed as real as the rainforest. Razor sharp rocks sliced the current everywhere along the river's path. Rapids crashed against one another in dangerous patterns. His chances of swimming to safety were not good.

A stalk snapped and the first of his pursuers burst from the jungle. The armed man stumbled into the small clearing.

The gun kicked in his hand. The shot caught his intended assassin off guard. Forward momentum carried the victim over the edge of the small ravine and into the river below. The body did not resurface.

A report from the bush forced him to one knee. His foot struck the black ticking box; its metal surface squealed across the jagged rocks just before crashing into the river below.

He pulled the trigger again and started running along the ledge of the canyon in the direction he could best call downstream. Others would be upon him soon.

Tearing back into the jungle was an option but he was certain that the natural obstructions would eventually lead him to a literal dead end.

The only option was the river. He ran closer to the edge of the cliff. His running became irregular. The broken ground made it difficult. Loose rocks fought the soles of his boots for traction. Untamped soil shifted beneath each step. Still, he needed to build up enough speed to land in the center of the river where he hoped it was deepest.

His personal countdown began at three. Somewhere at two-and-a-half a bullet caught him in the leg and turned him in mid-flight.

Squeezing the trigger with disciplined control, he fired his last round. The open slide on the gun signaled the futility of pulling the trigger again.

Soil and rock dug in to his back as he crashed to the ground and nearly slid over the face of the ledge.

Scanning the wall of weeds and plant life, he couldn't see who had fired the shot. Sadistic laughter escaped the underbrush. His shot had been in vain. They had fired from cover. He had fired carelessly.

Blood flowed from the wound in his leg, and only now he noticed how badly the vegetation had treated him. Flaps of skin hung like half-punched tabs in a hundred places. The blood loss from the scratches and gashes easily matched the flow from the bullet hole in his leg. The mere sight of it all caused his strength to wane.

With what strength he had left, he pushed himself over the edge and into the water below. As he fell, he prayed he would miss the rocks. A brief burst of foam marked his entry. It was washed away a moment later.

The current bounced his battered body between rocks and eddies. He fought to find the surface, but could not determine up from down. Gravity had control of his body and it now fought the current for the right to drown him.

The pull of the river ceased as he was forced against a rock. The river pushed him fast against it; the weight forcing what air was left from his lungs. He struggled and turned allowing the current access to his back. The change in dynamic rolled him away from the boulder and to the surface.

Gasping at the air, he desperately tried to fill his lungs. Water rushed into his open mouth as he rose and fell with the waves. He rotated his body in the surf and saw the large boulder only moments before he struck it.

Everything went black. His wounds no longer hurt.

* * * * *

Five men emerged from the rainforest. They, too, were covered in sweat and blood from the pursuit through the jungle. They reached the edge of the cliff and peered into the river. They saw nothing but froth.

2

Green turned to white as the waves of the Gulf of Mexico broke against the yacht's twin bows. Their force smacked with a hollow thud on the fiberglass shell and resonated deep within the ship. Outside, the hull glistened and answered each crest with a thwack that sounded not unlike the slap that was about to knock the drink from Paul Nelson's hand.

He grinned at the girl. It was a grin that was charming, crooked, filled with confidence and a recent deep whitening treatment. Slurring words had not yet become a problem, and if she liked what he had to say, he would confess that he couldn't possibly be as drunk as she assumed he was. If she balked at his advances, however, he'd blame it on the booze.

"So, Katherine? Are there any beaches on these islands?"

The smoldering look was worth the stupid question.

"Of course, Mr. Nelson." Dark hair flowed to her shoulders and framed a slender face. Her blue eyes narrowed as he leaned in close. A gust of wind blew a strand of hair into the corner of her mouth. She brushed it away.

Paul misinterpreted the gesture; he embraced the imagined opening and leaned in closer.

"Paul. Call me Paul."

"I'm sorry, Mr. Nelson. I'm not allowed to do that. As I was saying, the chain features over four hundred islands, each with at least a quarter mile of white sand beaches reclaimed from Wassaw Sound."

"What say you and I find a nice, secluded beach when this millionaire's tub toy puts in?"

"I'm sorry, Mr. Nelson. I can't do that either." Katherine Bernelli stepped to one side, opening an avenue of escape. She caught the eye of another investor, nodded, and began to make her way across the yacht's expansive deck.

Paul stammered as she made her way around him. The charm wasn't working; he may have to resort to flattery. He studied her as she moved across the deck, but as she walked his concentration swayed away, gently, back and forth in a tailored white formal gown.

Katherine reached another guest and smiled. Paul was amazed; the title Investor Relations Specialist no doubt called for her to smile always; yet he could find no trace of falsity in her eyes.

Paul tried to read her lips as she spoke to a gray-haired old man in a tailored suit. They were all old men with tailored suits. And, with the exception of one man he nicknamed "Johnny-Just-for-Men", they all had gray hair, which they would undoubtedly refer to as silver.

The swig of Jack registered in his throat, and he moved toward her with a new plan and a new grin.

"Yes, Mr. Hale, I believe the tractor did arrive on your island just yesterday. And, may I say the plantation you built is utterly stunning."

He smiled back at her as he sipped from a mimosa. "It's always been a dream of mine to live a simpler life."

"A hobby farm does sound like fun. And, the soil should be perfectly suited for most any crop."

"Oh, I'm not going to grow anything. I plan to just sit on the porch with a drink."

"Oh, but the tractor?"

"Young lady, you can't have a plantation and not have a tractor."

"Of course. Well, it is beautiful. Is there anything else I can do for you?"

"Fetch me another drink, sweetie?" He polished off the mimosa and handed her the empty glass.

She smiled, nodded, turned and sighed. The smile faded. She walked into Paul.

"Look, Kat. I'm sorry if I came on strong. I know that your job is to make nice to all the rich and powerful here and that you're just humoring me. But, I want you to know that I'm not like all these other guests. Look at that guy." He pointed with his rocks glass to no one specifically. It ended up being "Johnny-Just-for-Men," who was engaged in conversation on a Bluetooth headset.

"He can't relax. He's always on. Look at his posture. He's standing straight up. His arms behind his back, chest out. Classic steepling. It's as if he's dressing down the troops right here.

"But, I'm not like that. I'm not going to posture and preen. I'm up front with who I am. I'm relaxed. I'm fun. For example, underneath this suit, I'm wearing a t-shirt that says 'Hooray for Boobies!!!'"

She was startled. For the first time he saw a shift in her eyes from professional to woman.

"It has three exclamation points, Kat. Three! Let's see 'Mr. Buy/Sell' over there match that."

"What exactly is it that you do for Mr. Bennett, Mr. Nelson?"

"My file didn't say?"

The smile returned. "You don't have a file. Mr. Bennett has a file."

"Cool. What's it say about him? I could use some dirt."

"I'll admit you're both quite a mystery to us. We didn't even know that you planned on attending this event."

"C'mon. I'm sure there's a file that says something."

"The file tells me that your boss is one of the largest investors in the project. But, it doesn't mention you."

"I'm Mr. Bennett's Minister of Finance and Dirty Limericks. Wanna hear one?"

* * * * *

Steve Bennett stepped from the opulent cabin of ImagiNation's luxury ferry in time to retrieve the dropped rocks glass. Ice tumbled from the glass as his friend stumbled across the deck.

Katherine Bernelli's smile was gone. She scowled at Paul.

Steve could instantly see why his friend had risked the assault. She was beautiful. Even in her frown, it seemed as though she was smiling at him. Perhaps it was the eyes that always smiled.

Katherine noticed Steve and her rage turned to panic. She spun and rushed through the crowd – excusing herself frantically as she went.

Steve steadied Paul. "Limerick?"

Paul nodded, "It didn't work."

"Maybe it's not the right limerick."

"No, it's just not the right girl."

"Why don't you sit down for a while and try to stay out of trouble?"

"Why don't you make me, Steve? Quit trying to talk me down. I was just having a bit of fun."

"Why here?"

"Here's where I am?" Paul smiled and took the rocks glass from Steve's hand.

"This may not be the best place to be yourself."

"You always say that." Paul waved him off and turned to look for the bar.

"It's always true."

"I'm not trying to impress anyone." Paul rubbed his cheek. "Well, the girl yeah, but now that's out."

Steve looked around. What attention the slap had drawn had dissipated. "I'm just saying, calm down."

"You need to calm down, Steve. And quit trying to fit in with these people. You're richer than most of the fools on this boat. That's all the impressing they need."

"I'm not trying to impress anyone."

"Well you're trying hard not to piss them off."

"You should try as hard." Steve watched the Investor Relations Specialist duck around the yacht's superstructure. "Just sober up. I'll be back."

"You sober up."

"Good one, Paul."

Steve followed the woman. Paul refilled his drink.

Paul caught the eye of a slender woman in a black dress. Her age betrayed her as either a rich man's assistant or trophy wife. He studied her for a moment and tried to determine which. There was no nametag on her breast, so he decided to go in for a closer look.

* * * * *

Steve Bennett excused his way through the crowd; he stepped around the waitstaff as they shuffled about, making sure not to step between any guests engaged in conversation. Most of the guests on deck looked at him with a smile, but he could sense the puzzled thoughts behind each one.

Despite his own tailored suit, Steve Bennett stood out as an impostor.

Every glance sized him up and placed an impression in the observer's mind. They all knew his name and his story. His name had been featured on agendas in countless board meetings; his story had been told at cocktail parties. These people had suddenly become aware of him. He was now related to them all through investments and holdings, endowments and proxies. But they were all strangers to him.

Steve Bennett pulled back his shoulders and quickened his pace. He made it through the crowd and turned toward the back of the yacht.

* * * * *

Wake folded over wake behind the ship's powerful, water-jet engines. Katherine stared at the turbulent waters and watched the waves roll into one another. Fear had given way to anger and she stood without moving. Even the rocking of the boat beneath her feet did not affect her sheer force of will.

"Excuse me, Miss?"

"Get bent," the words were soft. "I liked this job."

"Pardon?"

"I slap your friend. I get fired. That's how it works."

Steve approached and leaned with his back against the rail next to her. He crossed his arms. The waves of the wake churned faithfully in time to the thumping of the engines.

"That's how it works?"

"My boss is in the salon. Go. Get it over with." She fought back a tear. After all the glad-handing she had done it was unfair that a latecomer would be the undoing of her career.

"I've heard the limerick, Miss. I'm surprised you only slapped him. He's limped home from several bars for that one."

She lost interest in the waves and turned to Bennett. He wasn't tall. He wasn't slim. He looked uncomfortable in his Armani, even though the fit suited him perfectly. There was a reassurance coming from his pale blue eyes that comforted her.

"You're not going to have me fired?"

"I think you're doing a fine job."

She wanted to smile but turned back to the wake "It doesn't matter. Once my boss hears, he'll let me go anyway."

"No. He won't." Steve stood from the rail. "I'll talk to him. I'll tell him the limerick."

This time she did smile. "You're not serious?"

"Who's your boss?"

"Warren Baxter."

"Which one is he?"

"You are new here."

He shrugged and looked away.

The ferry slowed and sank deeper into the water as the twin hulls settled into the Gulf. Steve was caught off guard and had to grab the rail to maintain his balance.

She giggled to herself. "Does your friend really have a shirt that says 'Hooray for Boobies?'"

"Yes. But he also has one that says 'No Fat Chicks.' So it's a toss-up as to which one he is actually wearing."

Katherine smiled. "I'll take you to Mr. Baxter myself, Mr. Bennett."

"Call me Steve."

"This way, Steve." She offered her arm.

Steve smiled and moved to take her arm, when a movement caught his eye. A wall of water rose from the Gulf. The wash crested the railing of the ferry and found its way deep into the fibers of his new suit.

Katherine was caught in the deluge as well. Dripping, she rushed back to the railing and shouted after the smaller craft that had caused the splash.

"What was that?" Steve tried to shake the wetness from his fingertips.

"Pacifists." She spat the sarcastic comment from her lips.

"Are you sure?"

"It's an environmental group. They've been protesting the site since before there was even a site." She pointed and Steve's gaze followed.

The boat sped away, but not before Steve caught the middle finger being thrown his way. Two of the men stood on the rear deck. The shorter of the two looked frail and overeducated. He had thrown the finger as he laughed and mocked the wet couple. The second did nothing. This solid figure only stood with his arms crossed, glaring at Steve. As this stocky man locked eyes with Bennett, Steve could swear that over the whine of the smaller boat's engine, the roar of the sea, and the booming of the diesel-powered water-jets, he heard the man growl.

"Environmentalist? That guy looks like he could hug a tree into mulch."

"We were told that it's a new group that formed in response to ImagiNation's plan to build the island chain. That never made sense to me. We say the Tortugas Banks in the literature just for a point of reference. We're not that close. And, even at that, the reclamation engineers went out of their way not to endanger the reefs or the national park."

"He looks like he wants to hurt me."

"They buzz the yachts and occasionally play chicken with some of the dredging ships. Aside from this kind of crap," she shook more water from her hands, "they're harmless."

"I don't know," Steve continued to stare at the man in the boat. "They don't look harmless. You don't get that big playing hackey-sack."

Steve broke the stare and turned to look at Katherine. Her white gown had turned transparent. Blushing, he removed his drenched suit coat and tossed it around her shoulders.

Puzzled, she looked at him and then made the connection.

It was Katherine's turn to blush as she pulled the jacket closed and turned to leave. She turned back. "Thank you, Steve."

3

"This is ImagiNation!" With the flair of a practiced showman, carnival barker, or pickpocket, Warren Baxter stood aside the windows of the main salon and presented the man-made islands on the horizon. The applause was inebriated and enthusiastic.

Paul sipped his drink as he studied the view. From his seat near the bar, he could see seven islands – their man-made nature evident only from water muddied by unsettled sediment. He knew from the website that there were three hundred and ninety-seven others just like them.

The audience erupted into conversation as everyone clamored to the windows for a better look. Paul remained near the bar as the line thinned out.

"Where did you put the bags?"

Paul turned, "Good news, Steve. They thawed out Walt Disney. This guy Baxter and his world of ImagiNation put on quite a show while you were gone."

"What did he say?"

"The bad news is that the name ImagiNation isn't just a placeholder. He really seems serious whenever he says it. He even looks to the sky when he says it, as if it were a stroke of genius. Other than that he didn't say anything that wasn't in the prospectus that Campbell sent us. He just added extra thanks for everybody's money. You got a personal nod."

"It's not my money."

Paul sighed, "It wasn't your money. And, it wasn't your investment. But, now it is your money and your investment. These are your islands, man."

Steve took the drink from his friend's hand and drained the glass.

"You still don't get it, do you, Steve? You're rich! Rich beyond belief. You need to start believing it." Paul ordered another drink. "You've got so much money now that your job is to watch your money. And, even at that, there's too much to watch. Lucky for you, I'm willing to help." Paul took the drink from the bartender.

"Lucky me." Steve took the drink from Paul's hand and took a sip.

"You'd better believe it. Do you think I actually enjoy eating the finest foods, driving the fastest cars, and spending my working days traveling to brand-spanking-new paradises? No. I do it for you." Paul ordered another drink.

"Thanks." Steve finished the drink and placed the glass on the counter.

"The fact that you pay me to do it doesn't hurt either. But, I'm starting to look at my job as making sure you realize what you have. And, that you start enjoying it. Take the new suit you're wearing. You can't be comfortable in that. Hey, you're wet."

"I'm glad your watching out for me."

"What happened? You fall overboard?"

"Never mind. Where are the suitcases?"

"I'm not really sure. I gave them to some guy and that was several whiskeys ago."

"Great. I'm going to go stand on the bow until I dry out."

"I'll join you. I could use a better view of the islands."

"Paul? If I was to ask you, as my self-appointed Director of Spending, what you thought of this investment. What would you say?"

"Steve, it's brand new dirt. They don't make this stuff anymore. These islands are going to sell like mad. Forget all this 'ImagiNation, your imagination is the limit' crap, and you've still got a brand-new paradise, with the very large checks being made out, in part, to Steve Bennett of Delacroix Industries. With a friendly fraction going to me. Plus, it's a great excuse to drink girlie drinks without feeling all gay."

"Just go find the suitcases and bring me another one of my fine new suits. And, tell Baxter I need to speak to him. I'll be on the bow playing king of the world." Steve took Paul's drink from his hand and walked onto the deck.

"There's a bar right here Steve!" Paul ordered a fourth replacement whiskey from the bartender. "Some manners, huh Isaac?"

"My name is Roger, sir."

"Of course it is, Isaac."

* * * * *

The wind blew cold through his wet clothes. The whiskey was warm in his stomach. And the thought of a multi-billion dollar fortune in his name made him shiver. In the end he felt that they all balanced out.

"Mr. Bennett?"

Warren Baxter extended his hand; the smile on his face was broad and genuine. Bennett offered his hand in return.

"Warren Baxter. I am delighted to finally meet you, Mr. Bennett."

"A pleasure, Mr. Baxter."

"Warren. I insist."

"If you say so, Warren."

"I do. I hear you wanted to speak to me. And, I wanted to speak with you, Mr. Bennett."

"Steve. I insist."

"Of course."

"I wanted to talk to you about Miss Bernelli."

"Yes. An unfortunate situation."

"I would prefer it if no action was taken against her."

"She did slap your friend."

"My friend deserved it."

Baxter smiled.

"He told you the limerick, didn't he?"

Baxter nodded. "Vulgar but amusing."

"So you understand?"

"Consider the matter closed."

"Thank you."

"No, thank you. Thank you for coming. Your last minute appearance was a pleasant surprise."

The conversation devolved into smiling and nodding. Steve was more uncomfortable than ever. He regretted that small talk was something he would have to learn.

"It's a nice boat. Ship?"

"This is nothing. I actually got it off of eBay, would you believe it? An old ferry we had gutted and refurbished at the last moment. Actually, if you can keep a secret, some of the paint is still wet.

"But, this ship is nothing compared to what you will see over the next couple of days. My dream of heaven on earth has come true on these islands. And you and the other investors have made it happen. I can't thank you enough for that."

"It was my father's investment. Not mine. Though I must say that I am beginning to get excited about it."

"I'm glad to hear it. I can't wait for you to see it all. The resorts built here are the finest in the world. Rivaling any you may have stayed in."

"Well, I would hope so, since up until six months ago I was staying in Super 8's or anything next to a Shoney's."

"Right, I'm sorry. This must all still be a dream for you."

"It's a little difficult to get used to. I've been kind of easing myself into the role of heir."

"My boy, you can't ease yourself in. You have to jump right in. And tonight you will experience the lavish lifestyle you now deserve. The main resort of the central island has no equal. You'll finally get a taste of the good life, Steve."

He forced a smile to match Baxter's, "That's great, because so far it's really just been a lot of paperwork."

"A terrible necessity. Tonight you will see the fun side of being filthy, filthy rich."

A hostess approached and spoke softly to Baxter.

"Of course, I'll be right there." He turned back to his guest, "Excuse me. I'm needed in the radio room."

"Of course."

"I look forward to talking later. I'd love to hear more about you and your father." With this, Warren Baxter, the dreamer behind the islands that now surrounded them, turned and walked back towards the ferry's bridge.

"That makes two of us, Warren."

Paul came around the corner with a dry suit in one hand and a drink in the other; he almost knocked the older man off of his feet.

"Ah, Mr. Nelson. Thank you for the amusing story about the girl from Huntsville."

"No problem, Baxie." Paul winked at the hostess as she lead Warren Baxter to the radio room then brought the suit to Steve.

"Here, I grabbed the other Armani and the fancy pants that came with."

"Forget the Armani. I'm pretty sure I packed a pair of Levi's."

"Yes! It's about time." As Steve walked away, Paul tore off his suit jacket and shirt and threw them overboard leaving only his 'Hooray For Boobies!!!' t-shirt exposed to the bright Gulf sun; it's glow-in-the-dark design charging for a long night.

4

David Jefferson had held the stare until the man in the wet Armani turned away. Confident he had made himself clear, he turned and climbed into the rear seat of the runabout. His large frame dropped deep into the cushion for the rest of the journey back to their ship.

The Rainbow Connection sat at anchor on the far side of the man-made islands created by Warren Baxter and his myriad investors. The old freighter was a former merchant ship that had spent most of its life crossing the Atlantic. Now it held, not cargo, but men dressed in hemp shirts, cargo shorts and Birkenstocks.

All it had needed was a quick cleaning and a few hand-painted rainbow flags to suit the new owners who were little more than a website and non-profit form. They had organized in response to the announcement that ImagiNation would undertake the largest land reclamation project in the world. Within weeks of the development's press release they were steaming towards the project.

They arrived shortly after the first surveyors, and irritated those plotting the islands with laser pointers. They played chicken with the dredges as the ships tried to empty hoppers full of sediment into the green-blue waters of the Gulf of Mexico. And they kept careful records of everything they had seen.

The ship's on-board database contained numerous files on everyone who stepped foot on the islands. Terabytes of data stored detailed information on anyone associated with the project: builders, sailors, financiers and more. One file was missing from the ship's computer.

"Who's the punk?" Jefferson asked the man settled in the bench seat next to him.

"I don't know." Conner Fredericks was small and wiry; a camera hung from his neck. "He must be new. I managed to snap a few shots of him before we soaked them. I'll start putting something together when we get back to the ship."

Jefferson's eyes were cold. "I don't like not knowing things. These islands are almost finished. Hell, half of them are mostly developed. I don't want any surprises."

"As soon as I get back. I'll run him through the system. Promise."

"No surprises, Fredericks. We've waited too long."

5

The islands of ImagiNation rose from the surface of the Gulf of Mexico. Each was elegant and finely cut, shaped and carved from the earth as if struck by a jeweler. The lush vegetation stood in stark contrast to the brown of the mottled water below and the blue sky above.

Very little development could be spotted from the deck of the ship. What few rooflines that could be seen were obscured behind landscaped clusters of trees.

The one exception lay directly off the bow. A single island, larger than the rest, was the foundation for a grand hotel. A Mediterranean-style building rose several stories above the flat waters and towered above the surrounding properties.

"Master Key, the central island, will house our main facilities: the resorts and casino, the spa, shopping and services.

There is even a race track on the island." Katherine stood between the two friends, but leaned closer to Steve as she spoke.

"Race track?" Steve, finally dry, had, at Paul's badgering, asked Katherine to give them a personal tour as the yacht sailed through the island chain.

She nodded, "*Road and Track* is actually doing a photo shoot there next week."

"It must be a popular place."

"The hotel itself isn't set to open for a couple of months. Mr. Baxter insisted that the investors see it before the public."

"Are we staying in the hotel? Because, I'm not sharing a room with the rich kid." Paul threw a thumb at Steve. "He snores."

"No, Mr. Nelson, you're not. But, due to your late arrival you will be asked to share a private villa."

"Private villa? I guess I'll manage."

"It's beautiful." Steve was lost in the sight of Master Key. "Is it the only completed island?"

"No. Most of the islands have been completely reclaimed. Only one outer cay is still being formed. Many of the private islands have already been developed."

"That's a lot of tiki huts, Kat." Paul had slowed his drinking but still leaned on the rail of the ferry for support.

"Hardly. You should see these estates. Each island is developed by the owner to his or her own personal tastes. Even the shape of the island is customizable. One investor brought a castle from Europe. He's having it rebuilt stone by stone. He calls it Avalon."

"A castle on an island...where do you put the moat?"

"Many of the investors here are owners. Maybe you should ask them." Katherine had been happy to agree when Steve asked her for a personal tour. But she had been certain that his friend would have found a cozy bunk to pass out in by now.

"Maybe I will." Paul turned to look back into the crowd on the deck. "Avalon, eh? So I just have to figure out which one of these guys would be into his own sister."

"This may sound like a stupid question, Katherine. Are any of these islands mine?" Months before the lawyer had simply handed Steve a brochure with a dollar amount scrawled across the top. It didn't specify what the money had bought. They may have said more but the inheritance had come as such a shock and the paperwork in such a barrage that he couldn't remember much of what the lawyers had said.

"Yes. But it's the final unclaimed island. Your father passed before he finished designing it."

"Oh. I guess I'll be in one of the huts then."

"The villas are hardly huts. Each is appointed with the latest technologies, finest linens..."

"You're starting to sound like the brochure."

"I'm sorry. I spent the last three weeks poring over the literature to get ready for today. But, you won't be alone on Master Key. Most of the guests here today are staying on the island."

"Are their paradises not ready yet?"

"Mostly, no. Power will be supplied from the central island. But, it has yet to be run beyond the core islands. So, unless they've put in a generator, they'd be sleeping in the dark. Plus, not all of the people here are owners. They're merely representatives here to watch over the investment."

"I'll resign myself to the super-premium hut then."

She laughed and placed her hand on his arm. "You'll have to excuse me. We're not far from docking and I need to see to the arrival. But, I'd be happy to show you around later. There's so much to see. And not all of it's in the brochure." She turned and walked away, slowly.

Paul and Steve each looked after her longingly as she disappeared in to the main cabin.

"She laughed and touched you," Paul said.

"I know."

"What you said wasn't funny."

"I know."

"I think she likes me, Steve."

"I think you're an idiot, Paul."

* * * * *

"Come, everyone. I can't wait to show you what we have done. Together we have all built paradise!" Warren Baxter led the crowd down the composite gangplank onto the central dock at Master Key.

"Every island is unique. Each investor has complete control of his or her environment. Vegetation, development, even the shape of the island itself can be changed to fit their vision of a perfect paradise. Of course you all know that. Many of you, or your employers, have already crafted that paradise from your very imagination. But, what I want to show you is the rest of the amenities available to our residents and future guests."

Steve and Paul fell to the back of the crowd, each hesitant to step from the gangplank. Steve felt out of place; Paul was drunk. An army of porters forced them to move from their perch as the uniformed force moved up the ramp to retrieve the luggage.

Baxter continued, "This is Master Key – the largest and central island in the archipelago. On it stands the grand hotel and casino. Here you will find shopping that rivals Rodeo Drive, spas offering the most indulgent treatments and so much more. We have brought the world's finest goods and services to ImagiNation."

Steve looked at the boats that lined the marina. Yachts and sailboats sat empty. Sailed by their crews to the island chain, they awaited the arrival of their owners. Even the fleet of water taxis bobbed in silence against their moorings.

"As you know, the only way to ImagiNation is by boat or seaplane. And, the only way between the islands is by private boat or water taxi. Around us sits a small portion of our fleet. These vessels will take visitors and residents between their destinations.

Because, even though we have it all on Master Key, there is so much more to do and see."

"The old guy is turning in to Dr. Seuss on me. When do we get to the hammocks, Steve?"

"You were the one that talked me into this. Remember, Paul?"

"Spread throughout ImagiNation are specialized islands: sporting fields, water parks, we even have a game preserve with guided safaris. You can see the world from Master Key." With this Baxter paused for effect. The only sound was slight lapping of the waves in the protected harbor and the rustling of the palm trees. Birds chirped occasionally. Steve wasn't sure if they were migratory, imports, or animatronics, but they remained true to the 'world of your own' effect.

An engine tore through the silence.

The crowd turned to face the disturbance. A large patrol boat roared into the harbor.

"Ah, and security. ImagiNation offers the best in security to ensure the safety and privacy of all of our guests." Baxter said.

A security officer leapt from the boat as it drifted into its berth. Despite the heat and humidity of the day, the guard wore a full uniform that consisted of a dark long-sleeve shirt and matching pants. No badge or patch presented the man as island security, but the large pistol at his side, and the shotgun slung around his neck, were more than enough to distinguish him from any guest on the island.

The boat was moored. Another man in uniform stepped from its deck. He addressed the crowd.

"My apologies, Mr. Baxter. We didn't expect you so soon."

"That's quite all right, Chief. Our pilot surprised me as well. He put the ferry through its paces and got a new top speed out of her. Shaved ten minutes off of our time."

"Still, I'm sorry for the dramatic entrance."

"Ladies and gentlemen. This is our Chief of Security. Mr. Richard Savage. Chief Savage leads a small army of officers hired to protect the property and privacy of our residents and guests. Their experience makes them more than qualified to chase off the paparazzi, discourage a peeping Tom, or sink a pirate ship." Baxter laughed at his own joke. "Though the likelihood of that is slim."

The security chief nodded but didn't laugh at Baxter's weak attempt at humor. A scar ran through his right eyebrow and intensified the hardness in his eyes. He looked to his men, who scrambled to secure the equipment from the patrol craft. He turned back to the crowd.

"Ladies and gentlemen, welcome to Master Key. If there is anything myself or my men can do to assist you, please do not hesitate to ask."

"Do your men carry rifles all the time?" An older woman nodded to the weapon across the man's chest and took half a step behind her husband. It was unclear if she was more afraid of the weapon or Savage himself.

"Shotgun."

"Same thing."

"No, ma'am. As I mentioned, you arrived before we expected you. My men will only have their sidearm at all times. Rifles and shotguns are mission specific and will be kept out of sight of the guests. As a matter of fact, my men will remain out of sight, as best as possible, unless needed. Each of them has extensive training in weapons and security, and are only here for your safety."

With this said the security personnel on the boat left the dock and disappeared into the landscaping that surrounded the dock.

"Cool," Paul leaned into Steve, "ninjas."

The older lady had relaxed little; it was the security chief that frightened her. She stared at Rick Savage as she spoke. "Warren? Is all of this really necessary? Guns and fast boats? Is it really paradise with all of this? Can't you just give your men pepper spray or those laser things?"

"I assure you ma'am, my men are the best. Each has years of milit..."

"I wasn't speaking to you, Mr. Savage." The braver her tone, the further she stood behind her husband.

Baxter raised his palms, "Mrs. Pritchard, I assure you that we are in good hands here. And, whereas we are in paradise, we must assure that all of our guests are safe from any possible threat. With this much wealth in one place, ImagiNation may seem a tempting target were it not for Chief Savage and his men. And as he stated, the 'big guns' only come out when absolutely necessary.

"Now, if you will please proceed down the path. The porters will take you to your rooms and our brunch should be ready for us in the hotel in an hour." Baxter turned to Savage as the porters hefted the passengers' bags and led the guests down the path to the hotel.

"Mr. Savage. What is with the shotguns?"

"A hippie boat needed a hole in it."

"Please, watch the labels. Just make sure they don't interfere with the tour again. They buzzed the ship on the way in. They gave one of our guests quite a soaking."

"They'll be stuck on their ship for a while. My men put their launch out of action."

"Very good. Try to keep your men out of site. And keep up the good work."

Steve and Paul stood on the dock and watched the crowd, and Warren Baxter, disappear around the bend. They each shook their head in disbelief at the choreographed movements of the porters and laughed.

Rick Savage also shook his head is disbelief. "Pepper spray. Yeah, right lady." He stepped back onto the boat to retrieve his gear.

"What do you think about the security, Paul?" Steve mocked Mrs. Pritchard's arrogant tone.

"I think with a name like Rick Savage he had to enter private security. You know? Or porn. I'd have picked porn–if it were me. But, I don't know what his options were. Maybe he's got a little..."

"I think it would be best if you gentlemen caught up with the rest of the group." The security chief had come from nowhere. One moment he was on the boat; the next he was behind them.

Paul jumped.

Savage was relaxed but there was a menace in his expression. It was the scar. The change was subtle at first; but as the security chief glared at Paul the scar across his brow darkened to a deep crimson.

Steve shuffled off, trying to hide a laugh as Paul and Savage locked eyes.

"Sir?" Savage gestured to the path.

Paul stood silent, too brave – or too drunk – to let go of the stare. Finally he smiled and pointed to the holster on the security chief's hip. "I have a gun. It's not as big as yours though."

Savage said nothing. There was no change in his breathing, no anger in his eyes – only the deepening red of the scar.

"So, I'll see you at the brunch then?" Paul stepped around the broad shoulders of the security chief and walked to the end of the dock. He turned the corner of the path.

"I hate the rich." Savage said as he heaved the bag of gear over his shoulder and strode down the dock to his office high in the Grand Hotel of Master Key.

Protests of old metal filled the deck of the Rainbow Connection with squeaks as the hoist set the launch on the deck.

Water flowed from the holes in its hull; seawater spilled across the deck, washing fiberglass threads over the sandal-clad feet of the crew. Five rounds from the security team's shotgun had caused the craft to list, forcing them to limp back to the Rainbow Connection. The launch was crippled, but it could be repaired. The ship's crew began to measure and cut patches before the boat was completely drained.

The Rainbow Connection's engineer stood back to inspect the damage. "It'll be all patches soon. I'm getting a little tired of these Bondo jobs. How long are we going to let them do this?"

"If we get the launch fixed in time, we should be able to hit the island tonight." Jefferson spit on the deck. "Is Reynolds back with the Zodiac yet?"

"Not yet. He should be."

David Jefferson looked off at the nearest island; a marvel to some, trouble to him. An entire ImagiNation rising from the gulf was unnatural in its truest sense. He shook off the disgust. "Give me an ETA on repairs when you can. I'm going to grab a bite to eat. What's in the mess for lunch?"

"Steak."

He cast one more glance toward the islands and then stepped below to eat.

* * * * *

Fredericks sat at a table on the far side of the mess hall. The man was so tall that he hunched as he shoveled food into his mouth with one hand and worked the keyboard of a scratched and beaten laptop with the other. He spotted Jefferson and waved him over.

Jefferson sat across from him and let the bulk of his weight rest on the table. "What've you got?"

The wiry man spun the laptop around to face David.

Jefferson leaned in closer and saw an online profile that outlined the man they had splashed. He squinted.

"It's Steven Bennett," said Fredericks.

"Bennett? He isn't supposed to be here."

"He's here."

"This isn't good. What's his background?"

Fredericks turned the screen back around and pulled up a second file. He scanned the information and called out the highlights. "Steven Bennett. 28. Get this? The kid's a billionaire. He inherited it from his father."

"Another rich kid playing with Daddy's money."

"No. It says here that he didn't even know he was rich until several months after his father died."

"They weren't close, huh?"

"Not at all. Bennett didn't know whose kid he was until the lawyers tracked him down."

"Still. I thought he wasn't coming."

Conner Fredericks shrugged.

"Doesn't matter," David Jefferson stood and shook the concern out of his expression. "It's too late to do anything about it now. We go ahead with the plan." The hemp shirt had risen up his back; he pulled it down over his massive frame and made his way to the serving line to get some steak.

* * * * *

Captain Richards stroked his silvered beard. Each gray hair marked a day running cargo across the Atlantic. This job was his retirement run – easy and safe. All he was hauling now was dirt – earth dredged from the bottom of the Gulf Intracoastal Waterway. Scoop it up, steam to the Tortugas Banks, and pump it out; that was all there was to it.

He still had the nerves for stormy weather, but spending most of the job in the protected river way wasn't causing him to complain. If there was anything to complain about it was the distance of the haul. Dirt was everywhere. Soil lined the bottom of the gulf. Yet, they were hauling it hundreds of miles from the Intracoastal.

The reason had been made clear to him. The reclamation project could only proceed in the Tortugas Banks if the project served a greater purpose. Forming new islands near a national park would have been impossible if the company had not agreed to dredge 90% of the reclaimed earth from the clogged transportation route.

The logistics frustrated him, though not enough to add more gray to his beard. At his age he should have been getting his legs back under him ashore, but the money had been substantial enough to keep him off the porch and man one more helm. And since the company had provided him the latest dredging ship to command, he had very little to do other than give orders to the crew and say, "very well."

There was a time in his life when such little involvement would have made him restless; but that time was twenty years ago. His wife had her eye on some property in the mountains of Colorado, far away from the sea, and, whenever the ship was pointed in the right direction, he would kick back and think about the large log home she told him he was going to build her.

She would decorate the home; there would be no stopping that. His grandchildren would run and play and break the nice things he had brought her from his many trips across the world. But that's what grandkids were for.

A wood shop out back would be his escape. And that would be his. All his. Dark and quiet, it would have a giant padlock on the door that could be locked from the inside and out.

A chime brought him back from the Rockies as the hopper neared capacity. The sluice foamed as soil filled the large tank in the center of the ship.

"80 percent, Captain." The crewman working the dredge's pumps was one of the best in the world. The company had made up for the distance by hiring the best crew possible. "Another half hour and we'll be ready to head back to the chain."

"Very well," said Captain Richards. "Very well."

7

The bags hit the floor and Paul hit the couch. "Wake me for lunch."

"It's brunch."

"I don't want brunch," Paul draped his arm over his eyes. "When they put away the crepes and break out the burgers, you'll know where to find me. I need a little booze-snooze if we're having cocktails tonight. I want to be in peak condition."

"Do you ever think that you drink too much?" Steve sat his bag down and dug his wallet from his pocket.

"No, but I know that you talk too much."

"You don't..."

"See? More talking."

Steve tipped the porter. Paul began to snore.

Tuning out Paul's raspy gasps, Steve strolled through the private villa. He was still not accustomed to being surrounded by luxury, and examined everything with the apprehension that touching anything in the room would result in a holler, a leer, and a reminder of a you-break-it-you-buy-it policy from an unseen maternal figure lurking in the wings.

The villa was larger than the exterior had led him to believe. Two master suites, each with a private living area, were connected by common living space and dining area that overlooked the beach. The kitchen was large enough to feed more people than could possibly occupy the space. Steve wondered if the stovetop or oven would ever see use.

The bathrooms were marble and spacious. When he spotted the bidet he decided to step outside.

He continued through the master suite to French doors that opened onto the beach. Thick-cushioned patio furniture lined a wooden deck around a fire pit that popped to life as he approached. A TV mounted under the pergola streamed the financial news. The sand began a few feet beyond it all.

Steve lit a cigarette with the Zippo he always kept in his fob pocket. He snapped the lighter shut and studied it. There was no logo, no design. Not even an engraved sentiment marked the smoked chrome finish. It was chipped in places and the lighter itself was pocket-worn on the corners. There was nothing fancy about it all. It fit comfortably back into the fifth pocket of his broken-in Levi's. It had felt odd bouncing around loose in the suit pants he had worn most of the day. It was reassuring to have something back in its place.

Past the porch was Paul's desire; he had fallen asleep only steps away from it. Two palm trees framed the beach in front of Steve. Between them, a hammock rocked gently in the breeze. He walked to the palms and rolled into the hammock, distributed his weight diagonally across the Brazilian design, and stared out beyond the beach.

Islands surrounded him. Roughly one hundred-fifty feet separated each cay, but from his position, there was a beautiful blue canal stretching onto the horizon and beyond. He took a deep breath and held it for a moment. Exhaling with a slow continuous breath, he closed his eyes. The beauty remained, even behind closed lids. He inhaled again, slower this time through his nose and pushed the air out through his mouth.

The scent of crisp sea air and new construction filled his senses. The hammock swayed in sync with his breathing. Then he opened his eyes, rest his head, and felt terribly uncomfortable relaxing in a hammock on the most exclusive beach in the world.

Maybe with enough time in the hammock, he thought, he could get used to being rich.

Months earlier, Steve sat at his desk with the copy of the will in his hands. On the computer screen were several open tabs of information on Henri Delacroix. Image searches had revealed pictures of the man, always shaking somebody's hand for a ceremony, fundraiser, or business deal.

Campbell was trying to locate more personal photos, family photos, or anything that would give Steve a glimpse into his father's personal life. It was proving difficult.

There was little personal information about the man to be found on the web. Everything he could find was about his father's company, Delacroix Holdings; there was nothing about the man himself.

All the articles said the same thing – he had been the third richest man in Canada at the time of his passing; there were no known heirs.

Steve was thankful for this. Campbell had been diligent in hiding Steve's involvement from the media. There was no doubt that it would have to be addressed, Thomas had informed him, but it could wait until Steve was better prepared for it.

The impending media frenzy frightened him. He envisioned it being covered not unlike Power Ball winnings, only worse. What would he say? How would he answer the inevitable question: "how does it feel?"

The money terrified him. People would accuse him of profiting from a stranger. The world would know him. Money like this didn't change hands without fanfare.

He hadn't even told his boss about it yet.

Paul had told everyone. His best friend had quit his job the day after Steve signed the papers, and began daydreaming what position Steve was going to hire him for.

The list had been extraordinary: sports car tester, date pre-screener, personal film and TV critic. His friend's enthusiasm was overwhelming.

Paul had planned out that first day in writing, and left the to-do list on the fridge in the apartment they shared. It had included: order premium cable channels, call ex-girlfriends and rub it in, quit job in legendary fashion, book flight to Vegas, throw out toilet paper, buy flushable wipes, get a smoking jacket, and a litany of other new purchases.

Steve didn't have the heart to tell him that he was considering passing on the money and donating it all to charity. It would be easier.

He had wanted to take some time off to think it over, but his vacation request had been denied. HR had been of little help when he requested time off for grievance.

The head of the HR department had asked how he knew the deceased. When he answered honestly and said that he didn't, she gave him a strange look. It was justified, but he simply told her to forget the request and wandered back to his cube where he loaded the bookmarks about his father.

"What are you doing?"

Stewart Reynolds had been his boss for only a short time, but had already made a habit of surprising his staff. He stood at the entrance to Steve's cube and grinned. The middle manager took great pride in sneaking up on his underlings.

"Hi, Stew."

"Is that PowerPoint going to be ready for the presentation Monday?"

It was Wednesday. If Steve started working on it on Monday, it would be ready Monday. "Monday's not a problem."

"See, you say there's no problem, but I see a problem." Reynolds reached across the desk and turned Steve's monitor around. "I see you surfing, not working."

"I was just looking something up."

Reynolds removed his hands from the monitor; his fingers leaving orange fingerprints on the white surface. The biggest problem with his rub on tan was that it seemed to rub off just as easy.

"Henri Delacroix? I don't think the PowerPoint is about Mr. Delacroix. Or am I wrong?"

Steve said nothing.

"Get back to work Bennett and save your online crushes for after hours. Oh, and that reminds me. Call your roommate and tell him you'll be late tonight." Stewart Reynolds turned and walked silently out of the cubicle doorway.

A moment later Steve heard his voice from the row over. "Prior. Do you have that report for me?"

"Yes, sir. I just sent it to you. Would you like a print out?"

"Of course. Good work, Prior." Reynolds continued on his way.

Steve stared at the monitor. The orange smudges drew his eye away from the screen. He looked back at the will in his hands and made his decision.

Paul had performed a skit in his office's lunchroom during the Monday morning company meeting. He had told Steve that it was an inspired piece, drawing allusions to several classics. For the epic poem portion of the second act he boasted that he had even managed to rhyme 'orange' with 'up yours'.

It had seemed excessive at the time, but now it held a certain appeal. Poetry had never been his strongest subject and he struggled for only a few minutes before giving up on the dialogue to a skit. Instead Steve walked over to the copier, xeroxed his middle finger and left it on his desk with a note that said, "see you."

9

Rick Savage found Warren Baxter on the balcony of his office. The office occupied the seventh floor of the Grand Hotel and the balcony opened to the beautiful world that Baxter had created. The elder man drew on a cigar and marveled at the view.

A rocks glass and a bottle of Scotch rested on the railing, three fresh ice cubes awaiting purpose from the amber alcohol.

Savage stepped loudly onto the balcony, announcing his presence with the heel of his boot against the tiled floor.

Baxter turned.

"You wanted to see me, Mr. Baxter?"

"Rick. Please sit down." Baxter crossed to the railing and grabbed the bottle of rum. "Would you like a drink?"

Savage waved the offer off and settled into a deep cushioned chair. "What did you need, Mr. Baxter? As you know, I'm quite busy now that we have actual guests on the island."

"Of course. A few things have come up and I want to make sure they are being addressed. First is this Rainbow Connection that's sitting by my islands. They've been quite a nuisance during the reclamation and construction process. We have tolerated this so far, but, as you say, we now have guests on the islands."

"Don't worry sir. They only had the one launch and my men put several holes in it today."

"You didn't fire on anyone did you?"

"No. The boat was empty, moored to their ship. No one was in harm's way."

"Good. I abhor even shooting the boat, but I don't want any surprises tonight. It is crucial that all goes well."

"Of course."

"Which brings me to my second point." Baxter filled his glass and emptied it in a swift movement. There was no flinch, no reaction to the alcohol as it shot down his throat. Years of drinking could preclude whiskey-face, but Savage knew that Baxter only drank the smoothest Scotches.

It was foolish of any employer to think that Rick Savage would take a job without gathering intelligence on them. Savage had researched Warren Baxter exhaustively. The man had made his fortune in coastal real estate in Georgia and the Carolinas. He had diversified as his wealth grew. Baxter held a controlling interest in multiple industries; he sat on the board of several more. The man had enjoyed the benefits of wealth for decades.

Before his financial rise, however, Savage could find little information about Warren Baxter.

Baxter poured himself another drink, "We have two unexpected guests, Mr. Savage."

"Bennett and Nelson?"

"Correct."

"They're a couple of winners."

"Now, Mr. Savage, they are our guests."

Savage nodded as Baxter tapped a half-inch of ash from the cigar and began to sip his Scotch.

"I have never met them; however, I knew Bennett's father. He was a big believer in ImagiNation and contributed greatly to its formation. His passing, a couple of months ago, was quite unfortunate. I spoke with the executor of his estate, a Thomas Campbell, about the young man who would inherit his fortune. He knew very little about the boy."

"It seems he's willing to let you keep his money. That's what matters, right?"

"Don't be so crass. This project relies as much on passion as fortune. This passion for ImagiNation is what I want them to experience."

"From what I've heard, you just need to keep serving Nelson booze and he'll be happy."

"My point is, Mr. Savage, that I was not prepared for their arrival. They drove up moments before the ferry left the dock."

"What? They didn't RSVP?"

"No," Baxter laughed, "and from the state they were in I'm not sure they even knew they were coming. They came rushing to the boat, Mr. Bennett schlepping his own bags, Nelson yelling to hold the 'dinghy'. They were panting for the first five minutes.

"But, now that they are here I want to know all about them, so that we can make them as comfortable as possible. I desperately want them to enjoy themselves."

"Shouldn't be hard in this place."

"You'd be surprised. It seems our new billionaire is having a hard time adjusting to his fortune."

"And Nelson?"

"Nelson seems to be the only reason that Bennett is spending any of the money. He seems more than happy to have access to the inheritance. An unfortunate problem with money, Mr. Savage, is that the more you have, the more friends you have."

"Well, as long as they're happy." Savage stood to leave.

"Mr. Savage, please. If you could, check with your sources and see if they know anything about the pair. My secretary's inquiries are limited to Google and I'm afraid it didn't turn up anything except a photo of Mr. Nelson at a Jack Daniels' party in a Dallas bar."

"How deep do you want me to dive?"

"Deep enough."

Savage nodded.

"Thank you, Mr. Savage. And, please, watch those protestors. Tonight must go as planned."

"There's no need to worry about tonight."

Warren Baxter turned back to the view, dipped the end of the cigar in his drink, and placed it back in his broad smile.

Savage turned and strode across the antique appointed office. He stopped at the desk, opened the humidor and retrieved a cigar. Its odor was sweet as he ran it under his nose. With a deft move he slipped it into his breast pocket. He gently closed the lid to the humidor and left the office.

Warren Baxter was once again facing the sea, and did not care that one of his prize cigars had just left the room.

* * * * *

Bennett couldn't remember falling asleep, and he awoke without opening his eyes. The sun was low in the sky; the rays beat through his lids and painted his vision red. The massive palm fronds above provided no shade. He squinted harder to block out the intensity of the light. The red faded. He opened his eyes. Paul stood less than two inches from his face.

"There's someone at the door."

Steve screamed and rolled over, backwards, out of the hammock. He hit the fine sand flat on his stomach.

"Then answer the door!" Steve put his hands down to push himself up. The sand scorched his palms.

"I would've answered it but I'm pretty sure it's for you." Paul walked back into the villa. "I'm going to take a shower."

The knocking continued as Steve slowly rolled over and sat up. A moment later, it was all but drowned out by the noise from the multi-jetted shower. Paul never closed the bathroom door.

Steve brushed himself off, and wondered where the sand came from. Katherine had mentioned Wassaw Sound but he had no idea where that was. He found himself marveling for the first time that the island he was standing on hadn't been there two years ago.

He hesitated to enter the living room covered in beach, but the knocking persisted; so he walked across the cool marble tile to the front door, taking large soft steps to reduce the spread of the sand.

"Steve?" Katherine's voice was muffled through the door. "Steve?"

The door opened without a sound; the hinges were regularly oiled to prevent rust and squeak. Katherine stood with her hand upraised, ready to strike the door again. She was beautiful. Gone was the gown from the boat. She now wore a pair of shorts and a loosely-fitted white linen shirt. The bleached white blouse stood in contrast to her olive skin and jet-black hair.

Steve quickly brushed the sand from his shirt and ran his hand through his hair to check for any hammock head that may have set in.

"Oh," she lowered her hand and noticed that he was covered in sand. "Is everything all right?"

Steve looked around puzzled, "Yeah. There's plenty of towels and everything."

"Not with the villa. You missed the brunch. And, the lunch. Mr. Baxter was concerned. And when your friend didn't show at the cocktail reception...even I got a little worried."

Steve looked around the room for a clock and then dug his phone out of his pocket. It was five o'clock.

"Sorry to worry you. I fell asleep in the hammock. Soothing motion, calming seas and all."

"What about Mr. Nelson?"

"He was taking a nap on the couch."

She shook her head and smiled.

He smiled back, "What?"

"The porter has come by several times. Last time he pounded on the door for fifteen minutes."

"Nothing wakes Paul from a booze-snooze."

"I just wanted to make sure everything was all right. I can get you copies of the presentations from brunch and..."

Sand dropped from his hair as Steve shook his head. "If I hear any more about how wonderful this place is and how my imagination is the limit I'm going to swim back to Key West."

She pouted in jest. "But it's my job to make sure orientation goes smoothly. You wouldn't want me to get fired would you?"

Steve leaned against the doorframe, "Haven't we done this already?

"Look, you want to make sure I get my orientation? Show me around a bit. I don't want to see another brochure, prospectus, or toothy grin from Mr. Make-believe." He turned back to the sea. "But, I am starting to really like this place. Those are some great hammocks."

"You're covered in sand. Clean up and meet me by the hotel in half an hour. I'll show you around." She smiled and turned away. He smiled back. When she was out of sight he closed the door and leaned his head against it.

"Told you it was for you."

Steve spun and saw Paul standing in his boxers rifling through a travel bag. "I think I forgot my deodorant. Where's yours?"

Before Steve could respond Paul had found the deodorant and was heading back to the shower rubbing Steve's Right Guard under each pit.

"I wouldn't want to offend anyone. Though it looks like I might be on my own tonight."

* * * * *

The Grand Hotel on Master Key rose seven stories and towered above all other structures in the ImagiNation archipelago. The white stucco exterior fed the sun back to itself, and gleamed with a reflection equal to that of the whitest sands.

The hotel stretched along the central northern end of the island with its back pointed to America.

Despite its size, the hotel did not dominate the island. Architectural details and the shape of the structure combined with creative landscaping to immerse the building into its surroundings.

Even the large ornate pillars that framed the main entrance seemed to blend in. They stood the full seven stories; each comprised of three spiraled spires. Steve guessed that the open space in between the individual spires aided in their unassuming presence.

He had showered and dressed in new shorts and a new shirt, reluctantly applied his borrowed deodorant and ran for the door. As it closed behind him, Paul had reminded him to, "Do what I would do. It's fun."

He had arrived early.

The extra time had allowed him to stroll the interior of the casino and hotel. The casino alone occupied half of the first floor. Baxter had planned for a great amount of action on its tables.

The lobby seemed to be carved from solid marble. Black and white sheets of the polished rock were laid seamlessly together, giving the tropical resort a chill. He shivered as his skin rippled in the cool, empty air of the lobby.

The other guests weren't as adventurous as Steve. With the exception of security details, he had seen no one during his stroll. Napping in the hammock may have caused him to miss the guided tour; still, the lack of visitors was odd. He assumed Warren Baxter had wrangled them into another theater for another speech.

The speeches had gone stale. If they were designed to make the investors and their associates feel better about their investment, they were having the opposite effect on Steve. He'd already seen all he needed to see in the sand and trees around him. It was an island paradise in the Gulf of Mexico where one had never existed before. No amount of fantasy or dreams-come-true monologues was going to make the ownership any more desirable. It was time just to enjoy the islands.

Katherine arrived in an electric cart that bore the ImagiNation logo. Steve smiled; his father's fortune had opened up a lot of opportunities. This was his favorite so far.

She smiled at him from behind the wheel and patted the seat next to her. "Hop in, and your orientation will begin."

"What's the plan?"

The cart whirred and lurched into motion. Steve looked at his hostess, leaned back in the seat and smiled. She focused on the path ahead of her.

Hot, humid air turned cool as the breeze from the cart flowed around him. He gazed around as they passed the various structures on the island. A moment later he spotted more people; the islands' guests were gathering for another speech.

"Is this a trap?" Steve waved a hand at the crowd.

She smiled and turned onto a path that led them away from the audience.

They passed an intersection of the narrow cart paths and a second cart fell in line behind them. Steve waved to the two security guards in the cart. They did not respond.

"Not too friendly."

"But, professional. Which would you rather have protecting you?"

"I never really felt like I was in any danger here."

"See?"

Katherine took a sweeping left on the cart path; Steve grabbed the roof to keep himself in the cart. The black asphalt path widened to two cart lanes and a walking lane on either side. The security guards fell further behind them.

Moments later they were amongst a group of buildings that lined the meandering path. Architecturally, the buildings resembled a ski village. Each was larger than most nestled mountain hamlets could afford, but the inspiration was clear.

Designers' names marked the stores. Display windows featured the latest fashions from around the world. Steve counted no less than four jewelers, not including the watchmakers Patek Philippe, Blancpain, and Glashütte.

There were several cafés, a nightclub or two, and multiple stores and boutiques lining the narrow avenues and side streets. Katherine sped by them all.

"Aren't you going to point out the sites?"

"It's all in the brochure."

"So where are you taking me?"

"You'll see."

She turned towards the west end of the island and the setting sun.

10

The law offices of Thomas Campbell were pristine. Every folder was filed away each night before he left, and the mahogany furniture was polished to reflection by the next morning. Much like the older man, the offices were prim, proper, and presentable to the most refined clientele.

The attorney slid one final folder into his drawer before reaching for the only light that illuminated his office. It was the Bennett folder.

He smiled as he tucked it away. For more years than he could remember he had managed the affairs of Steve's father. Henri Delacroix had been a businessman to the core. The shrewd investor and marketer had amassed a fortune like none other in the Canadian provinces. Lumber, oil, plastics, the richness of Canada's natural resources had given the man his start. Soon after, he moved into publishing and venture capitalism.

Pharmaceuticals, tech firms, and construction projects deepened his portfolio and his pockets. Art and antiques, even classic cars, enriched the man's extensive accounts. It seemed nothing he touched would spoil.

This was not without careful consideration. Everything Henri Delacroix acquired was carefully researched, analyzed, and dissected until he was certain there was a fortune to be had.

It had come as a great shock to Thomas when he discovered he would be contacting young Steven Bennett of Dallas, Texas, to hand over the fortune and the company that his father had built.

Delacroix had always taken great care of himself. Daily runs around his estate in upper Ontario would keep any man fit. And the adventures he pursued in the rare time he took off certainly kept his spirit young: safaris in Africa, hiking through the Alps, sport fishing, and any other adventure that could be arranged by a travel agent or outfitter. But, in the end no matter of good health could save him.

The accident was tragic. A drunk driver crossed the road and met Delacroix head-on. On this rare occasion, he had been driving himself. Had he been in his Rolls with his driver, there was little doubt he would have survived the wreck; but that day he had felt the need to indulge his desire for excitement.

German engineering was a passion and the Porsche was one of his favorite acquisitions. One Henri truly enjoyed. He collected traffic citations like trophies, each recording a new top speed.

The true irony of the accident was that he was stopped at a light, idling the GT2, when the minivan crossed over into his lane and ended his life.

The accident was tragic. A drunk driver crossed the road and met Delacroix head-on. On this rare occasion, he had been driving himself. Had he been in his Rolls with his driver, there was little doubt he would have survived the wreck; but that day he had felt the need to indulge his desire for excitement.

German engineering was a passion and the Porsche was one of his favorite acquisitions. One Henri truly enjoyed. He collected traffic citations like trophies, each recording a new top speed.

The true irony of the accident was that he was stopped at a light, idling the GT2, when the minivan crossed over into his lane and ended his life.

With so much invested in his dear friend's life and work, Campbell found it difficult to process the will. Instead he turned to his associates. He managed his associates through the bulk of it, scrutinizing the smallest details, but never taking the full document in. This was how it proceeded, until he learned of the boy. News of an heir was difficult to believe. He had known Henri Delacroix for more than thirty years and, even though Campbell suspected that the man had many children throughout the world, he was surprised to discover that his old friend was aware of them. He had never spoken of the young man; he had never reached out to the boy.

Thomas was quite sure the boy would be as shocked to find out that he had a father in Canada, as he was to find out that he was now in the upper ranks of the Forbes list.

For this, Thomas resented Steve. That the son who never knew the father should take on the rewards of an empire built by a great man was unjust. But he had no choice – it was his client and dear friend's final wish.

The search was easy enough. He knew the boy's name and the mother's name. The circumstances, however, were left out of the final instructions. It merely stated that Steven Bennett would inherit Delacroix Industries and Henri Delacroix's personal fortune.

Shock was mild in comparison to the boy's reaction. Campbell contacted him in person. He wanted to be there to see the look on the brat's face when he heard the news.

Everything he had learned about the boy was in line with his imagination. Not an exceptional student. Honors classes with a consistent C average, a college education, and then several jobs that led to no distinct career path. This boy had been given everything and applied himself to nothing. To cement Campbell's hatred, he wanted to see the smirk on the lad's face and verify Steven Bennett's pettiness.

The apartment complex was in a northern suburb of the city and held no distinction from the other ten he passed on the drive in. He huffed with each step as he climbed the flight of stairs and rapped firmly on the door. He heard fumbling inside the apartment for several moments before the door opened. The boy was just as he had pictured him: a smug look on his face, arrogant, and lazy; he leaned on the doorframe and looked Thomas Campbell up and down.

"I didn't do it."

"What?"

"Huh?"

"Mr. Bennett, I am Thomas Campbell, the executor of your father's estate. I regret to inform you that your father, Henri Reneé Delacroix, has passed on."

"Reneé?"

"I can see you're obviously shaken by the news, but we do have some business to attend to. Your father left his entire estate to you." He spoke more quickly than he would have to anyone else. His normal approach would have been consolation, compassion, possibly a hand on the shoulder and then, days later, the settling of the will. But he wanted to see, to prove to himself, that this boy was unworthy of the Delacroix legacy.

"How much?"

Americans, thought Campbell, "Your father was a billionaire."

"Are you serious?" A grin betraying his greed grew across the youth's mouth. He gasped and Campbell incorrectly detected bourbon on his breath. It was whiskey. "Wow! That's incredible."

Under his breath, and well under the screaming, Thomas said, "Brat."

Then aloud, "Your father was a great man. I'm sorry for your loss. But, we do have much to discuss."

A voice from the back of the apartment sounded a question, "Who is it?"

The grinning youth shouted back, "Some guy that says 'about' funny. He's says your dad is dead and you're filthy rich."

Steve Bennett came to the door.

"We're rich. Well, you're rich. But you can hire me for something or other. I don't work cheap." Paul headed back into the apartment.

The look on Steve's face was framed by ashen skin. His mouth was not quite closed, yet not quite open. His eyes didn't seem to respond to the sunlight as he stepped into the doorframe.

Thomas Campbell's pedestal of pride crumbled and his shoulders sank as he saw the features of his dear client and dead friend in the young man before him. The calm blue eyes did more for Campbell in verifying the rightful heir than any number of blood tests ever would.

He could see the boy was shaken and sincere. Steve spoke slowly and softly. "You knew my father?"

Campbell hung his head. He had blamed the boy for not being in his father's life. But it was obvious, that it was not the boy to blame.

"Mr. Bennett. I am truly sorry for your loss. Your father was a great man and a dear friend. I regret having to deliver this news, but I did want to do it in person. I understand that this is a difficult time, but there are matters we need to discuss. I will be in town for a couple of days." He reached into his coat pocket and pulled out a business card.

"I would be happy to answer any questions you may have. My office in Toronto can always reach me if you want to talk."

"Toronto?"

"Yes, sir. You're father was a Canadian."

Steve looked vacantly at the card. He stared at the name but couldn't read it. The address was a blur to him.

His best friend, Paul, broke the silence. "Hey. That means you're part Canuck."

"I'm truly sorry, Mr. Bennett." Thomas Campbell walked down the steps of the apartment feeling two feet shorter than when he had climbed them. Shame was cold in his stomach, and the heat stinging at his neck was embarrassment for accusing a stranger of not caring. Steve's only fault was in not knowing his father. And it was quite clear that the absence of family in his life had not been his fault at all.

Steve stopped him, "What was his name?"

"Henri Delacroix."

"Henri?"

Thomas Campbell walked back to his car and began to shake.

* * * * *

The room at the W hotel was not Thomas' style. His secretary, who always insisted that he get with the times, had booked it for him. Ultra-modern and stark white, the building felt cold to him; and as low as he was feeling he needed some mirth. He went to one of the hotel bars, and found even less solace in his drink. The "Ghostbar" was also ultra-modern and filled with the thin veneer of the Dallas nouveau riche. The long room was packed with people, and no two looked different.

He had just finished his drink, and made a mental note to remind his secretary that he was too old to try new things, when his phone rang.

The BlackBerry in his pocket was another new thing he detested, but, unfortunately, found necessary. It was a call. Not an email or text. A call. He pressed the answer button and held it to his ear.

"Mr. Campbell?"

"Yes. This is Thomas Campbell."

"If it's not too much trouble, sir. I'd like to talk about my father."

"Of course. I'm at a place called "Ghostbar," though I can't imagine why. May I suggest someplace quieter?"

"Please. I can't stand that place."

Thomas Campbell smiled as he and Steve Bennett, the son of a friend, made plans to meet in a quieter and more dignified place.

* * * * *

Thomas Campbell sat in his Toronto office as he remembered that day. They had talked for hours. The money finally came up at the end of the conversation. Thomas brought it up. Steve felt like he didn't deserve the money and insisted that it wasn't his.

The only way to further the execution of Henri Delacroix's will had been to remind the young man that it was what his father had wanted.

He tucked the folder into the drawer and pushed it shut. Steve's reluctance to accept his inheritance had persisted. It was only through due process and Nelson's badgering that he finally accepted it. This trip to the islands was a big step for Steve; Thomas wondered if perhaps he was coming to terms with the money at last.

Thomas turned off his desk lamp, leaving the room in darkness, and made his way home. He sincerely liked Steven Bennett, and hoped that he was enjoying his time on the tropical paradise that his father had helped build.

11

With a splash, the launch dropped into the water. Two crewmen in the boat unshackled chains and moored the craft to the retractable steps of the Rainbow Connection.

"The patches aren't completely dry, but they should hold well enough." Arnold Gibson completed his cursory inspection and lowered a section of the deck back into place. He nudged it flush with a rubber mallet and a couple of strikes of his heel.

"We won't be long." David Jefferson cradled a submachine gun in his arms.

"Aren't you taking an awful risk?" Gibson pointed to the H&K in Jefferson's arms. "Pacifists don't carry weapons."

"So we've become eco-terrorists. It's not a stretch."

"David. It's not..."

"This is my operation."

"I know. But, I've been with you a long time. I know how much this means to you. Don't lose sight of the big picture. You can't be seen..."

"Everybody in!"

Four men enshrouded in black clambered down the ship's boarding steps and piled into the launch. Each took an assigned position in the bow and on the gunwales. One fired up the engine as David stepped inside.

"Just make sure and run the pump," said Gibson. "Island security has put so many holes in the hull that I can't even guarantee I found them all. And remember what I said."

"Let's go." David Jefferson cast off the mooring line as the engine of the dark craft screamed to life. And as the sun touched the sea they moved off into the islands of ImagiNation.

12

Water arced from the rear of the boat as the Sea-Doo Islandia skimmed across the water. The vessel's shallow draft made the jet-boat the perfect inter-island transport. The archipelago's islands had been plotted and reclaimed in a pattern that reduced the wave activity within the chain, and allowed the smaller craft a smoother ride on the channels.

Steve watched the islands fly by as Katherine piloted the craft. The topography of each personal paradise differed according to the taste of the owner. However, every one was extravagantly landscaped to the last twig and berry. No single island was more than a year old and yet each looked as if the plants had taken root and sprouted years ago.

"We're almost there." Katherine had given no hint of where they were headed. Nor had she let up on the throttle since they had stepped in the boat.

"Where?" Steve had to shout to be heard.

"The edge of ImagiNation." She pointed ahead.

Steve laughed and she joined him.

"No, really." She watched the water ahead of the boat.

Steve looked over the bow of the small watercraft and saw the channel widen before them into the open waters of the Gulf of Mexico.

Katherine killed the engine and they drifted onto the beach of the southern channel island. It wasn't finished. The earth here was dark and thick, unlike the fine white sand that he had seen on every other island they had passed.

"Welcome to your island." She grabbed his hand and led him out of the boat. She ushered him onto the beach. He did not resist. Instead, he focused on the touch of her hand.

It was like in the old songs, before swearing and other dirty lyrics were allowed – a spark from the simple contact of this other person's hand delighted him.

She pulled him along to the western-most point of the island.

"Here's one of the best features," she was almost whispering. "It's the perfect island to watch the sunset."

"Why is that?" Steve shifted his feet in the claylike soil.

"No bugs yet, for one. Two," she pointed out to sea.

Steve looked back toward the western sky. Oranges and purples layered the horizon and the sun melted into the sea. All was quiet. The lapping of the waves disappeared. The rocking of the boat against the sand was distant to him. He stepped closer to the girl, and put his arm around her waist.

They watched as nature seduced them both and let themselves be taken in by the turn of another day.

"I try to come out here every night. It takes away the pressure and aggravation of the day. As if my troubles set with it. With all the unreasonable requests, endless paperwork, and dirty limericks I deal with, I like to come out here where I know I'm alone."

Steve turned to her. Her dark eyes smoldered as the breeze blew her hair across her face. "You're not alone."

"I'm as alone as I want to be."

He took her face in his hand and leaned in. Their lips met, their eyes closed, and the roar of an engine tore them apart.

Startled, they broke their embrace. The disturbance had come from the far side of the island. Steve turned. The beach was wide but not deep. It rose quickly to a slope not far behind them. The engine died and men's voices began to rise.

Still close, Katherine whispered, "I don't think anyone's supposed to be here."

"Guests?"

"They should all be at the dinner reception."

"Security?"

"Possibly. But I would be surprised. They usually stay on the patrol boats unless a private alarm has been triggered. This island is still being reclaimed and the work crew is on leave for another couple of days."

Steve crawled to the top of the muddy embankment and peered over its crest. A small group of men clad in black scurried about. Each was armed.

Across the island in the growing moonlight, Steve made out a boat with a black hull beached on the shore. Four men wrestled a large crate from the deck and shoved it toward the center of the island. Another man, weapon in hand, walked slowly toward Steve and Katherine.

Bennett scrambled back down the hill. His palms filled with wet clay.

"We should run."

They made it to the jet-boat quietly, the damp earth masking their footfalls. Katherine leapt into the cockpit of the Sea-Doo; Steve pushed it back out to the channel. As he pushed on the lip of the boat and pointed the hull upstream, the waves fought against them and threatened to force them back to the island.

"Steve." She wasn't whispering anymore. It was of no use.

The black clad figure stood above them on the hill of the beach. The barrel of his weapon was trained on Bennett. A slight shake of the gun indicated that the man wanted them back on the island.

Steve dropped his head in surrender and gripped the side of the boat until his hand turned white. Mud oozed from the lines of his palm. He whispered frantically. "Go, go, go, go!"

The wail of the Sea-Doo drowned out his voice.

Shock caused hesitation, and the gunman stumbled to find the trigger. The delay was enough for the water-jet to force the boat into motion.

Steve strangled the rail of the craft and tried to lift himself as far out of the water as possible. It wasn't far enough. The drag on his body turned the craft back toward the island as the water forced him below the surface.

There was a banging; he wasn't sure if it was gunfire or parts of his body being forced into the hull. His heels danced below the waterline. He gasped for air; water rushed into his mouth and forced its way into his lungs. He coughed and tried desperately to breathe as he strained his arms to pull himself free of the water's grasp.

Bullets chased after the fast-moving craft, but the gunman's window was short and his balance was off. Earth dug from the Intracoastal Waterway mixed with the pounding of the surf did not make for sure footing.

The jet-boat quickly turned the bend. The black boat was in the water and throttling up.

Steve suddenly found himself able to breathe and it was only then he realized that the boat had slowed. A hand touched his. He looked up to see Katherine motioning him into the boat.

"They're coming!"

Steve pulled himself over the side as she tugged at his shirt and shorts to help drag him in. With his feet still in the water he shouted at her, "Go!"

The sudden lurch of the Sea-Doo rolled him on the floor of the sun deck as the craft accelerated.

A series of coughs drove the seawater from his lungs. The sensation made him dizzy and he struggled to focus.

"They're right behind us," Katherine yelled as she wrestled the wheel back and forth to dodge bullets she could not see.

Steve pulled himself into the passenger seat and looked aft. The dark boat was gaining. Fast.

"Keep turning! Stay out of the main channel. I don't think we can outrun them!" Steve fumbled in his pocket for his cell phone. The touch screen remained dark. He rubbed its glass facing against his wet shirt and tried it again. "My phone is soaked. Where's yours?"

"There's no service here."

Frustrated, Steve shoved the iPhone back into his pocket. It was the one purchase he had actually enjoyed making with his father's money.

With every turn the nimble Sea-Doo pulled away from its pursuers, but with every straightaway they lost ground.

"This isn't good." Katherine screamed back at him. Her piloting skills were amazing. Though he was being tossed about the cockpit, Steve never felt that the craft was out of control. She was amazing; but it wasn't enough.

Katherine veered again into another tributary of the main channel. The primary causeway would take them to Master Key and the rescue of ImagiNation's security forces. But, out-powered, they had no way of staying in the channel for more than a short distance. If they weren't turning they were losing the chase.

Steve tried to stand and put a hand on her shoulder, "I have an idea. Head into the main channel."

"They'll catch up."

"Right. Trade places with me and hold on tight."

Katherine didn't budge. "Have you ever driven a boat like this?"

"No. But Paul made me rent a jet ski a few months ago."

She stared at him but did not take her hand off the wheel.

"Trust me."

Gunshots spouted geysers behind them. The dark craft was close. Only her erratic turns kept the gunfire from being lethal.

Katherine turned into the main channel and pointed the boat at Master Key. She let go of the wheel and traded places with the man she barely knew and put her life in his hands.

"Hold on tight," Steve crashed down in the pilot seat and gripped the throttle. It was already pushed to the stops, but he pushed it harder pleading for every bit of speed the engine had in it.

The shots came closer and Bennett swerved to cause a sway in the wake that would hopefully throw off their pursuers' aim. He straightened and pulled closer to the left bank of the channel.

The dark craft gained. Every moment brought their pursuers closer. The boat settled into the wake of the smaller craft and pushed the twin engines of the boat to overtake the smaller craft.

"Hold on, Katherine. They're almost on us."

The dark craft loomed behind them for only a moment. They had jumped Steve's wake and run wide, but quickly pulled alongside the jet-boat.

"Steve!" She could see the barrel of the gun pointing right into the cockpit of the Sea-Doo. Bennett was watching the other side of the boat. There it was.

Bennett cranked the wheel and reversed the throttle. The nose of the boat dove into the water throwing Steve and Katherine into the dash; the rear of the boat continued its momentum, trading places with the bow. The jet-boat came to a stop in a distance less than the length of its hull.

The dark and powerful boat sped past the stopped craft; the advantage of its speed turned against it.

Bennett thrust the throttle forward and turned into the channel tributary. They had gained time and distance on their pursuers, and Steve was not about to waste it.

Katherine let go of the handle grip. Her fingernails had cut the plastic coating, and her fingers hurt as she uncurled them. She gasped at the maneuver, knowing that the only person more surprised that it worked than her was the man behind the wheel.

She stared at him as he watched the water before them. She reached over and touched his hand. "I can't believe that worked."

When he glanced at her, she was smiling. "Me either."

They wove in and out around several islands before they felt confident enough to turn the engine off and listen. They heard nothing. They strained to hear the other boat's engine, but it seemed clear they had lost it in the chase. The Sea-Doo drifted, the gentle slap of the waves against the hull was the only sound. Steve reached for the key to restart the ignition.

The faint sound of a distant engine piqued their ears. It grew louder.

Steve scrambled to turn the key but lost it in his panic. He padded around the dashboard trying to find it.

The approaching engine roared and the boat came around the corner of the nearby island. Steve focused and found the key, but, before he could turn it, the boat was upon them and slowing.

It was different. Smaller. The boat drifted next to the jet-boat and the engine died. He had seen it and others like it at the dock – an ImagiNation water taxi. A figure appeared in the canopy's opening.

"You know boats are surprisingly easy to hot-wire."

"Paul! Thank god you're... you stole a boat?"

"You left me alone. I needed something to do."

"Is there a radio in that thing?"

"Yeah, but I think we're too far from Key West to get FM. And, you two look like you're doing fine without the soft music."

Steve hadn't even noticed that Katherine had grabbed his arm when they first heard Paul's boat. "Call security! We've been shot at."

"Get in the boat." Paul's constant smirk vanished. With the order given, he disappeared into the cabin.

Steve jumped into the ImagiNation water taxi, and helped Katherine aboard. As she boarded he asked, "Can you work the radio?"

"Yes." She moved forward to the cabin.

"Who shot at you?" Paul moved from one side of the passenger craft to the other, peering into the now black night.

"Don't know. They dressed in black, shot guns, and didn't give their names."

Katherine studied the radio and flicked the power switch several times. "Nothing. The radio is dead. Almost as if it's shorted out." She turned to Paul. Paul could feel her stare. Steve was glaring as well.

"Okay, so, maybe it's not as easy to hot-wire a boat as I thought."

"Back into the Sea-Doo. It's got to be faster than this thing. Chances are they still haven't a clue as to where we are." Steve ushered Katherine out of the water taxi. Paul moved forward to the cabin.

"Now, Paul."

"Go ahead. Just let me get this thing moving in the other direction. Then come and get me." He moved toward the cabin and Steve jumped back into the Sea-Doo. He waited for Paul to start the taxi's engine, and turned the key on the Islandia. The water taxi's engine roared and it began to move. A moment later Paul was in the water. Steve pulled alongside and fished his friend from the Gulf.

Paul wiped the water from his face. "At the very least, we should be a little harder to hear now. Tell your girl to keep it slow, and maybe they'll go for the noisy one." He settled into one of the seats behind the cockpit and was quiet. But, only for a moment.

"Only you could inherit a billion dollar fortune, come to paradise, meet a hot girl, and screw it all up by getting shot at. You at least did it first, right?"

"Dude."

"Just asking." His voice faded off. "Hoping. Whatever. It's been a while for you."

"Just shut up and start thinking what we do if they don't fall for your second boatman plan."

Paul reached behind his back and pulled a gun from a concealed holster.

"Where in the hell did you get a gun?"

"Academy Sports. As your Head of Security I felt I needed to be prepared."

"I never made you Head of Security."

"You never made me your Envoy to the Nudie Bar either, but I diligently fulfill those obligations at least twice a month."

"Put it away!"

"Calm down, Pinko. I didn't think you had a problem with guns."

"I don't have a problem with guns. I have a problem with you having a gun."

Paul tucked the gun back into the concealed holster. "It's not like I didn't practice with it."

"Don't let me see you with that again."

"We may need it Steve." Katherine pointed over the windshield to where a dark craft floated silently. A searchlight pierced the dark stretch of beach, and played upon the shoreline. "They're looking for us on the beaches. I guess they figured we'd take refuge on this overgrown island."

"What is this? A rainforest?" Steve stared into the dark mass of vegetation.

Katherine shrugged, "You rich people do funny things."

Steve shook his head. "Turn us around. Head to the next channel. We've got to make it back to Master Key.

13

The resort's premiere restaurant stood in brilliant contrast to its island location. Fine linens covered the tables. The waiters were dressed in tuxedos, and the walls were lined with amber panels gilded with gold leaf. The Amber Room had been meticulously recreated to match the original that once resided in Catherine Palace in St. Petersburg.

When Baxter had heard that the famous plundered treasure was being recreated in Russia, he contracted the artisans to make two – one for the palace in St. Petersburg and one for the hotel and casino on Master Key.

It had taken more than a simple request. The Amber Room, the eighth wonder of the world, was to have been a one-of-a-kind. Baxter spent the next few years hiring away the master craftsmen working on the project. One by one he built a team to create his own "one-of-a-kind" wonder.

Inside the room, tuxedos and black evening gowns filled, drifted, and mingled. The guests in formal attire popped like silhouettes against the luminescent walls. Even those representatives of the absentee investors were in their finest, as they mingled around the room expanding their networks and drinking heavily.

A string quartet played. Waiters and waitresses made their way among the crowd, holding aloft silver platters filled with the finest foods and gold crested flutes, pausing long enough only to serve, never to eavesdrop or observe.

Warren Baxter surveyed the room from the corner. Rick Savage stood close by with a radio headset that squelched in his ear.

Baxter smiled broadly; the power he had gathered in the room was amazing. Before him stood a group that represented an impressive percentage of the world's wealth and influence. He had done it.

Captains of industry, masters of finance, entrepreneurs, and visionaries milled about, basking in the glow that was the Amber Room and ImagiNation.

He studied the crowd.

A frown grew across his face and he spoke, interrupting Savage's conversation. "I don't see Mr. Bennett or his associate."

"No. You don't."

"I want them here." Baxter said.

"We don't know where they are."

"What do you mean? Everyone was to have a discreet escort."

"Everyone had an escort. Bennett was last seen with Ms. Bernelli. Nelson gave his escort the slip."

"The slip? Him? They must be somewhere on Master Key."

"Bennett left on what appears to be a personal tour. And then Nelson stole a boat," said Savage.

"Stole a boat?"

"Borrowed will most likely be the story."

"Find them and get them back here." He gestured to the gathering. "They simply must see this."

Savage glared and turned back to his radio. It squelched again; he listened intently. He turned back to Baxter, "I think we found them."

"Get them here."

The security chief did not run for the door. He never ran. Running conveyed panic. He nodded at Baxter's request and started to walk toward the doors.

"Chief Savage."

He stopped.

"It seems it would be worthwhile to keep a better eye on Mr. Nelson."

Savage nodded again, turned, rolled his eyes and left, barking commands into the radio as he made his way toward the docks.

* * * * *

They drifted away from the searchlight until they felt it was safe to run the engine. It wasn't until then that any of them felt it was safe to talk.

"They fell for it. My brilliant plan worked." Paul peered into the darkness behind the boat.

"Yeah, who'd of thought hot-wiring a boat would end up being a good thing? What the hell were you thinking?" Steve surveyed the quiet coastline of a nearby island.

"You're going to give me crap for this? You have a boatload of masked gunmen after you and I'm the one that made an error in judgment?"

Steve glared at his friend, "You're going to get us kicked off the island."

"It's your island, Steve. Didn't you see the paperwork? Without your money these islands would still be underwater."

"It's not my money."

Paul met his friend's gaze. "Oh, shut up you crybaby. There are a lot worse problems to have than being so rich. I'll give you an example: being chased by gunmen in a boat!"

"Two boats," Katherine's voice pulled them from their argument. The pair stared behind them fearing that the boat they had left behind had caught up. There was nothing there.

"Out front!"

They spun in time to see bursts of gunfire from the front of the boat. Katherine dropped and pulled Steve to the floor. Paul fell into the water as the unmanned wheel spun free.

The jet-boat spun wide and struck the beach of a nearby island. The engine was stuck at full throttle. Water streamed from the back of the craft as the water-jet engine forced the nose of the boat into the sand. Steve and Katherine were thrown forward in the deck seating. Steve leapt to his feet, found Katherine's arm, and steadied her. He could not see Paul.

"Paul?" Steve scanned the water.

His search was answered with gunfire. The boat's fiberglass hull splintered as it was raked with bullets. Bennett grabbed Katherine and pulled her onto the beach.

"Where's Paul?" He yelled over the shots.

She was shaken and did not respond.

"Run!" The voice was faint but Steve heard Paul yell the warning as the gunmen's boat beached up shore from their location.

Grabbing Katherine by the hand, he led them over the shoreline and into the island.

* * * * *

The water was warm but the sudden impact with the ocean had shocked Paul. He floated under the channel for only a moment before he swam for the surface.

The Sea-Doo was beached; its engine screamed as it tried to drive the boat further onto the sand; the back end swayed back and forth in the shallow water.

The black craft that had opened fire was turning towards the land. He grasped at the small of his back and retrieved the gun. Miraculously, it had not come dislodged in the fall.

Fire opened from the attacker's boat. Fiberglass splinters floated around him. Kicking furiously he drew the slide and aimed for the closest gunman. As instructed in his weekend class, he took a breath, exhaled half of it and stopped. He relaxed, stopped moving, and quickly sank to the bottom. They had never covered firing from a floating position. He resurfaced quickly, fired a blind shot and yelled to Steve to run.

Wiping the seawater from his eyes, he watched as Steve and his new girl ran over the breaker and toward the center of the island. Men clad in black leapt from the boat and pursued the couple. None of them seemed to be concerned or aware of him floating in the channel.

Paul realized that they might not have seen him, and if they hadn't found the water taxi, they might not have realized they were chasing more than two people.

"I have an edge," Paul whispered to himself. Land was close and he began to kick. He moved closer to the enemy boat. He didn't know much about taking on a host of armed gunmen garbed in black, but he had seen in countless movies that the element of surprise was a powerful one. It had always worked for Michael Myers. He approached the hull of the boat.

Sand filled his hands as he began to crawl through the shallow water. It was quicker this way and the fact that he could now stand and fire would certainly be another advantage.

The black boat's hull shielded him on his right. There was nothing but clumsily gouged footprints ahead of him. Open water was on his left. He guessed that there was a guard around the corner.

Paul braced his footing and prepared to spring his edge. Despite the surreal and dangerous situation that he now found himself in, he smiled a little. He loved winning. He started to stand.

"Don't move!"

The shout came from behind him. It was close, though still hard to hear over the whine of the beached jet-boat.

The guard had spotted him and lowered himself into the channel. He stood waist deep in the gentle waves.

"Stand up," the command was emphasized with the rising of a vicious looking rifle barrel.

Paul hesitated.

"I said get up."

Paul turned and got to his knees. He pulled his left arm from the water and kept his balance with his right still deep in the sand.

"Raise your hand slowly. A handful of mud won't stop a bullet."

Paul did as he was told and slowly raised the gun out of the water.

Expecting not a gun barrel, but a handful of wet beach, the gunman's eyes widened.

The first shot struck the guard in the shoulder, the second and third missed completely; the fourth entered the gunman's chest. The water swallowed the scream as he fell under the waves.

Paul reacted quicker than even he expected, and launched himself at the guard. The man struggled to stand as blood poured into the water. Paul kept him off of his feet, forced him to the seafloor, and stood on his back. The struggling stopped. He stepped aside and the body popped back to the surface. Paul took the rifle.

"Surprise."

* * * * *

Steve heard gunfire behind him and dove to the ground. He felt a pop and sudden pain in his upper thigh.

"Those weren't at us. Get up." Katherine pulled him back to his feet.

Steve blushed and tested his leg; it held and the pain faded. "I probably looked pretty stupid there, huh. I thought..."

"They came from the beach," Katherine pulled at his hand. "Run."

"The beach? Paul." He turned back to the shoreline.

Katherine pulled at his shoulder. "Keep running."

Steve ran with her. His panting became raspy. "We're going to run out of island. Pretty soon we'll be ankle deep in the next channel over."

Open terrain had greeted them on the island and left them with nothing but a few palm trees to hide behind. This changed as they reached the island's center. The elaborate landscaping was everywhere. Trees and outbuildings began to aid their escape. Steve vaulted a low-lying hedge line and stopped. Katherine landed next to him with a grunt. Waving her on, Steve flattened himself against the ground and the hedge.

Katherine crawled down the hedge line as Steve listened for the approaching footsteps. They were fast and heavy. A break in the cadence signaled their location. Steve shot his arms up just as a pair of combat boots cleared the hedge. His grip was solid. The eyes of the boot tore at his palms but he had his pursuer by the feet.

Momentum carried the gunman forward. With his hands firmly gripped on the rifle there was no stopping his face from hitting the ground.

Air burst from the gunman's lungs. A rush of blood poured from his nose. He did not try to stand.

Steve made a grab for the gun but it had slid from the man's hands into the darkness.

Katherine motioned frantically for him to follow her. Shelter provided by the hedge line, and knocking a man out, gave Steve a sense of control. His hopes rose. All of the crawling, however, was killing his knees.

Scrambling as quickly as quiet would let them, the pair made their way to the main home of the private island. The lights were out. He could hear no generator. The house was empty.

They crawled furiously. Steve's knees ached and he tried to keep the weight on his toes but this wore him out even more; he knew he would need his strength, so he let his knees suffer. After passing a lavish pool and cabana they reached the patio of the home. They still led the pursuers by half a minute. Steve stood, grabbed a patio umbrella and, wielding it like a lance, drove it through the mansion's patio door.

The glass did not give easily or quietly, but it gave.

He dropped the umbrella and grabbed Katherine's arm. "This way."

* * * * *

The gunfire from the beach had caused the pursuers to pause. It had not been precise, or close. Four of the black hooded men exchanged looks of astonishment and, after a moment, two were assigned to investigate the gunfire from the beach. The other two followed the sound of the broken glass.

* * * * *

Since he had become so proficient at hot-wiring, Paul was a little disappointed to find the keys in the black boat's ignition. He throttled back, and brought the dark craft off the beach. Then, for the third time in a half hour, Paul Nelson found himself jumping off of a perfectly good boat.

Guns drawn, ready to fill Paul with as many bullets as he would stand for, two men crested the breaker wall. Paul enjoyed the startled yells when they realized they would have to make a swim for their boat.

Paul swam toward the Sea-Doo, staying just below the surface of the water. He hid on the opposite side of the craft, and smiled as one gunman pulled off his boots and hopped toward the water in pursuit of his own boat.

The other guard turned toward the Sea-Doo and spotted Paul. He opened fire. Paul stopped smiling and dove. Bullets riddled the water; close. Too close.

One hit.

He felt the impact in his left forearm, and choked back a scream. He held the wounded limb before his eyes and expected to see the blood coloring the dark water around him. He thought about sharks, and cursed the Discovery network for their choice of programming.

There was no blood. There was a dull ache and he could feel a slight bruise forming.

Now that his eyes were open, he watched the bullets slow around him. They entered the water several feet away and slowed rapidly. Paul smiled again as he watched the trails. Beneath the waves, he began to hum *Remo Williams'* theme song.

He pulled himself back through the water and moved around the boat. He surfaced on the far side of the Sea-Doo with his finger on the trigger of another man's machine gun, and hummed even louder.

"Bum, badda bah bah. Bum, badda bah bah!" Paul emptied the entire 30 round magazine at his assailant; he hit him twice.

The gunman fell back to the white sand.

Paul tossed the machine gun in the boat and followed after it. He reached over the windscreen, throttled back and rolled back into the water. Two fierce shoves on the bow moved the craft back into the channel. He climbed back in, returned to the helm, and pushed the throttle to its stop. As he left, he tried to run down the swimming gunmen. He missed.

* * * * *

The umbrella pointed like an arrow into the home. Broken glass littered the marble flooring inside the darkened room. The chase ended here. They held at the shattered door.

"You go in the front. Watch yourself. There's plenty of places to hide in a house this size."

The gunman nodded and moved to cover the front of the extravagant home while he entered through the patio door.

* * * * *

Steve's legs ached. He hated running. He often claimed that he only ran when chased, but until now, he had never really been chased. His right leg screamed at him. He began to wonder what damage he had done in the fall. A cramp in his chest was nagging at him as well. Katherine was fit though. She pulled at his arm as they climbed the dune and fell back to the shore.

"We have to swim, Steve."

He could hardly catch his breath. But he nodded and pointed across the channel. He was steps away from collapsing in the channel when the Sea-Doo came into view.

The engine whined. Paul whined louder. "I just killed two people! Get into the stupid boat, now!" Paul ran the craft parallel to the beach.

Steve and Katherine rolled into the Sea-Doo. Paul had let little off of the throttle as little as possible; he shoved it back to full. The Sea-Doo's hull lurched from the water and pointed itself to Master Key.

Paul threw the machine gun and a full magazine at Steve. "We're heading back to Master Key. And, this time we're not stopping for anyone."

"Paul, are you okay?"

"Okay? Steve, I think I'm bulletproof!"

14

Seawater drained across the Rainbow Connection as the launch was lowered to the deck. The dark craft had not yet come to a rest when the men clad in black jumped from the boat.

"Get him down here," David Jefferson pulled the knit cap from his head revealing a bushy mane. His voice blistered with angry frustration. "Where's Gibson?"

The old mechanic, his friend and mentor appeared, "What happened?"

David Jefferson tore the black gloves from his hands. "Those bastards killed one of my men."

With solemn care, the body was lowered to the deck and placed on a stretcher. Not a word was uttered as the crew tended to their fallen brother. Jefferson pulled Gibson aside and whispered in his ear. "I'm moving now. This is all the justification we need."

"I'm not sure the boss will see revenge as justification to change the schedule."

"They fired first." David gestured to his fallen man. "We have to move before our cover is gone. The boss will see it my way."

"It's not time. You can't let your emotions run the operation."

Jefferson wasn't listening. He glanced once more at his fallen friend. "Clean him up and then gather the men. All of them."

"David, we can't move on the island now." Gibson said. "Their security will be on edge and those boys are hardly rent-a-cops. They'll be ready."

"They won't even see us coming." Jefferson stormed off, leaving a trail of water behind him. He had pulled the body from the ocean himself.

* * * * *

"You killed two people?" Steve couldn't tell if it was the situation or his opinion of Paul that had prompted Rick Savage to ask the question several times.

"Yes," Paul said studying the top of his shoe.

It had not taken long for the bravado and adrenaline to wear off after they had arrived safely at Master Key; shock had set in quickly. It had taken him less time to find a drink.

"And how many people did you kill, Mr. Bennett?"

"Maybe one. I can't be sure. I dropped him on his head." Steve sat in a plush armchair in the Chief of Security's sparsely decorated office and stroked the bandaged gash on his leg. His fall to the ground had broken the optical glass of the phone, bent the frame, and sliced his leg.

Savage looked to Katherine. "And you, Miss?"

"I didn't kill anybody." Her answer was weak. She stared at the floor.

Savage paced around his desk. Charts and maps lined the wall behind him. Tapping a large map of the islands he asked, "Where?"

Steve shrugged his shoulders.

Katherine looked up, "They started chasing us on 38."

"And you're sure it was the same boat that splashed you this morning?"

"It was a black boat," Steve answered. "Both of them were."

Savage shook his head. "The activist's ship carried a black launch. I doubt they could have patched it that quickly, but there's no reason to believe they wouldn't have another one."

The Security Chief rubbed his chin and studied the trio in front of him. Baxter's decree played in his mind; they had to enjoy themselves. Rick Savage sighed. "The important thing is that everyone is all right. My men will investigate 38. They'll recover the bodies for the authorities and try to confirm your story."

Steve leaned forward and pointed to the map. "The bodies aren't there. They chased us to another island."

"Which one?" Savage received only puzzled looks. "Could you identify it?"

"It's the one with the bodies." Paul said.

Savage felt blood fill the scar above his brow. A deep breath abated his temper as he considered his options. "You two come with me and help us identify the island. Ms. Bernelli, I'm sure that Mr. Baxter would like to hear the report first-hand."

She nodded and rose. She glanced quickly at Steve as if to say she was sorry and left the room.

The door closed and Savage turned back to Paul. "Give me the gun."

"No."

"I will not allow my guests to carry weapons."

"I'm licensed to carry this weapon within the United States, and we are still in the United States, right?"

"Yes. But, you don't need it."

"I already needed it once today, Rickie." Paul smiled broadly, enjoying the frustration in Savage's voice.

"We'll handle it from here."

"No."

"Mr. Bennett?"

Steve thought a moment and shook his head. "Mr. Nelson is my Head of Security and I would feel a lot safer if he were armed. Actually, he could probably use a reload."

It was Savage's turn to smile. "No."

* * * * *

A dozen armed men packed the deck of the security boat. Savage wasn't taking any chances against the Rainbow Connection and her crew. His men sat silently on the benches that lined the boat. Each carried a shotgun, rifle, or submachine gun. Each was clad in black.

Paul whispered to Steve. "These guys don't look like mall cops anymore."

Steve nodded. "I think it might be a good idea to stay out of their way when we get back to the island."

Savage sat down next to them. "We're not going to the island, Steve. We're going to the Rainbow Connection. That hippie ship has been giving me grief since I signed on, and your story, and that of Ms. Bernelli, should be more than enough to justify the assault. But, I am going to need you to identify the people who were chasing you."

"We didn't see them."

"A simple nod is all I need. We'll place them under arrest and hold them for the feds."

Paul laughed. "They just spent the night shooting at us. What makes you think they'll let you slap the cuffs on?"

Savage lifted the shotgun in his hand.

"No," Steve stood up, "I've had enough being shot at for one night. Take us back to the hotel."

Paul rose with his friend. "Yeah, you guys have a nice assault. I'm done playing war. We'd really like to go back and join the party. I'm sure there are a couple of women I haven't hit on yet."

"What kind of coward are you, Nelson?"

"The kind that would rather play with women than big burly hippies."

"I am so sick of your mouth, you little punk!"

"Punk?" Paul leaned toward Steve. "Get a load of Callahan here. He's probably got a big cannon, too." Paul looked back at Savage. The crimson scar blazed; his brown eyes turned black.

"Oh, I didn't mean it like that. I was talking about your gun, not your," Paul finished his statement by wiggling his pinky finger.

Savage raised the barrel of the shotgun and pointed it at the pair.

Steve and Paul stood up as the security chief moved closer.

"I am so sick of your mouth, Nelson. I was going to wait, hoping you would get caught in the crossfire, but I just can't take your shit anymore."

He pumped a shell into the chamber.

Paul jumped.

The boom of the shotgun was deafening.

Steve felt the wind leave his chest as he was struck with a force that he had never experienced. His feet lost contact with the boat and he flew over the railing and back into the water.

He sank. He felt a force pulling him under and away from the patrol boat. Struggling to resurface, he felt the resistance coming from an arm around his waist. It was Paul. His friend had tackled him from the boat and was now pulling him through the water.

Kicking to match his friend's stroke he ceased struggling and began to swim. It hurt. Paul's move had emptied his lungs, and they ached for air. The bandage on his leg filled with saltwater, aggravating the cut. Steve had to surface.

Grasping for the ocean's surface, he kicked furiously, each kick drawing more pain from the gash.

How deep had Paul pulled him? His vision started to fade around the periphery. Stars appeared before his eyes. Pressure filled his head. A final desperate kick propelled him upwards.

Air cooled his hand as it pierced through the dark gulf water. The sensation was greater on his face. He was dizzy and disoriented, but able to breathe.

He gasped and savored the salty air, but it was only sweet for a moment.

"There! There! There!" The voice echoed from the boat. Gunfire erupted. Where they really trying to shoot him? Steve tried to dive back under the water but found his body unwilling to obey.

The water was calm around him.

Rounds rattled from the security boats. Savage's men fired frantically into the night.

Paul broke the surface next to him and joined the confusion. "What are they shooting at?"

The roar of powerful twin engines drowned out the constant thrum of the security crafts inboard motor. The black craft screamed into view.

"It's the quote-unquote peaceful protesters."

"What are they doing here?" Steve was still gasping for breath.

"Distracting Dirty Harry." Paul grabbed his friend by the shoulder. "Swim."

They made for the closest island and left the security party to the fray

* * * * *

Savage fired at the black craft. He emptied the shotgun, drew his sidearm, and continued to shoot. The boat had come out of nowhere. Masked in the shadow of the surrounding islands, it bore down on his team from the darkness and opened fire.

Suppressing fire from his men caused the craft to veer away. He turned to grab a rifle and saw Bennett and Nelson swimming for the nearest island.

"Austin, Ramirez. Take two men. Take care of Bennett and Nelson."

Austin and Ramirez responded without a sound. Tapping two men on the shoulder, they made their way to the rear of the craft.

The four men broke from the firefight and slid over the side of the boat to pursue the guests.

* * * * *

Paul scrambled to the shore first. Steve followed. The gun in his hand still seemed out of place. Paul's awkward grip held the weapon ready as he scanned the beach.

"Steve, are you okay?"

Bennett was sputtering. Seawater dripped from the corners of his mouth. Coughing, he nodded. "Warn me next time you're going to do that."

"Fair enough. You warn me the next time some psycho security guard is going to kill us.

"He wasn't going to kill us."

"Then what was with the gun?" Paul watched the firefight rage at sea. The two boats turned so hard that they threatened to flip as the crews tried to gain the firing advantage.

"He was going to shoot you, maybe. I don't think me." Steve rose to his feet; his legs shook beneath him.

Paul placed his hands on his hips. "I'm hurt, Steve."

"He wasn't going to kill us. He was trying to scare you. You pushed him over the edge. The gun probably went off when you hit it." Steve pointed to the boat that attacked the security force. "They were going to kill us."

"I don't want anyone to kill me. I want to go home."

"We have to get back to Master Key." Steve found his footing and walked towards the interior of the island.

"We have to get back home. This place is nowhere near as relaxing as I first thought."

"Come on. Let's cut across this island and see if we can find a boat for you to hot-wire."

Paul moved past his friend and took the lead as they made their way into the heart of the dark island. He kept the gun in front of him while casting quick glances behind them. He crinkled his nose. "This island smells funny."

* * * * *

Katherine Bernelli stared at her feet as Warren Baxter set a cup of coffee in front of her. The ImagiNation logo presented itself on the curved porcelain as the coffee warmed the cup. Some of the liquid spilled over the top and settled into the ImagiNation napkin he had placed beneath it.

The Rorschach blot that formed reminded her of a pool of blood.

"My Dear, I'm so sorry for this. Had I known these environmentalists had tendencies toward violence I would never have permitted their presence." Baxter wrung his hands together.

"Why now? After all this time?" She wasn't asking him. He couldn't know.

Baxter placed a hand on her shoulder and was silent for a moment. He sighed deeply, "I don't know. The islands are nearing completion. Their complaints have fallen on deaf ears. It could be simple frustration running unchecked.

"Let's face it. Their cause was weak. Until the press releases began to garner us such attention, few people even knew the Tortugas Bank existed. Avid divers not withstanding, the location had to be one of the most unknown parks in the world.

"The coral is safe. The species are unthreatened. We are reclaiming the land from the Intracoastal Waterway. An effort that has been lacking, despite federal law, for decades. It's a great service.

"They have no outrage to exploit. No fire to fuel. They must have felt this was there last option."

"But why try and kill us?" Katherine began to shake. The day's events hit her harder the further they moved into the past.

Baxter placed his arm around her. "You're safe here, my dear. Mr. Savage will investigate. And your friend, Mr. Bennett, will be back shortly."

She said nothing. After a long moment she finally reached for the coffee.

"May I ask what you two were doing out there on your own?" Baxter moved across the room and poured his own coffee.

"I was just giving Mr. Bennett a tour of his island."

"But his island is unfinished. Although, it was a good idea to show him the reclamation process. It's still fascinating to me." Baxter chuckled, "I felt like a new father every time one of the islands rose to the surface."

"I was showing him the sunset."

Baxter nodded unsurprised.

"He seems like a nice man, Mr. Bennett. I met his father. His passing was a terrible thing. Sadder still was that he had never met his son. Did he enjoy the view, Ms. Bernelli?"

She smiled despite the terror, "I think so."

Warren Baxter smiled back, but it wasn't the showman's smile she was used to seeing; it was genuine. "There you go. It's not all doom and gloom. Now then, Let's focus on the work shall we." He took her hand and helped her to her feet. "If you feel up to it, it may prove the distraction you need. I still have an Amber Room full of investors with questions and, regrettably, some doubts and I need your help with the answers and reassurances. Let's not lose sight of what we are doing here. We are creating a perfect little world away from the violence and chaos of the mainland – in paradise there should be no tears."

"Mr. Baxter... "

"Please, Katherine. For me, put on a brave face and try to forget about this evening. You can rest assured that nothing like this will ever happen again. Enjoy the party. Have a drink. I'll be down shortly for the presentation."

Warren Baxter smiled to himself and puffed out his chest. The showman was back in the room. "It should be quite a night to remember. I feel in rare form and can't wait to address my fellow ImagiNation citizens."

Katherine smiled and decided that pouring herself into her work might be a good idea. She could fret later when Steve was back. They could get over the ordeal together. Perhaps while drifting off in the hammock he seemed to enjoy so much. Turning on her heel, she stopped herself short and turned back to Baxter.

She smiled, "Mr. Baxter."

"Warren. I think this ordeal has brought us to a first name basis."

"Warren. Could you let me in on the secret? What is the real name of this place going to be?"

The old man feigned offense, "You don't like ImagiNation?"

Her wry smile caused him to laugh.

"It is a little corny, I'll admit. The real name is still a secret and as the Chairman of ImagiNation I can not let the cat out of the bag just yet. But, I promise that you're going to love it."

Katherine shook her head, smiled, and left the ornate office. Warren Baxter smiled, turned and crossed to the windows.

The French doors to the balcony had been closed during their conversation. He felt she might be dismayed if she had to look upon the islands that had given her such a fright. He swung the doors open with great flair and stepped onto the balcony as he lit his cigar. In the distance he heard gunfire.

"Give those troublemakers hell, Mr. Savage."

15

The speedboat ambush soon evolved into a test of piloting skills as the two powerful crafts maneuvered for superior firing position. The roar of the engines overpowered the chatter of the gunfire as the two boats throttled and churned the water into froth.

The dark craft tried to gain the distance needed to maneuver, but found that the security boat was more than able to keep pace.

Rick Savage screamed into the radio for reinforcements; he relayed locations and instructions between bursts of gunfire.

David Jefferson barked orders to his men to keep the fire on the patrol boat.

This went on for minutes, each boat tearing a wake that crossed the other. Inside the boats, the men were thrown about, and careened off of one another. The pinball effect made firing dangerous.

The fiberglass hulls of each boat were gashed, as intended passes became collisions on the crests of the waves. Piercing shrieks screamed across the channel as the boats rubbed together.

It seemed an endless dance until a loud and hollow sounding "kathunk" echoed across the water. The muted bass note was followed by an explosion that tore a chunk from the security boat.

The craft began to list immediately, exposing the guards to their assailants. Still, they fought on. As the boat turned they stood on top of gunwales instead of behind them and continued firing.

Jefferson shouted another order; the M32 grenade launcher belched again and fired another 40mm round at the patrol craft.

The grenade tore the security boat in two. Bodies spilled into the Gulf as the craft was lifted from the surface and blown apart. The security force's guns fell silent. Their motors ceased roaring.

David Jefferson stood to his full 5' 8" height and surveyed the calming waters around the flaming wreckage; he saw no other movement beyond the quickly sinking boat. He nodded to his men and the engine of the black boat screamed back to life. "Let's go see what's shaking on the island."

16

The launch was still in sight when Rick Savage regained the surface. The first grenade had thrown him clear of the craft, and he had raced to the bottom of the channel, anticipating the second round.

Thankfully, the black craft had not lingered long. Striking the water had driven the air from his lungs, robbing him of all but a few moments to hide.

Smoke from the wreckage of his boat filled his eyes, causing them to water. The roar of the fire made it difficult to hear calls for help.

There were no voices in the wreckage. If any of his team survived, they would swim for shore. He would meet them there.

He spun in the water and spotted the closest island. He recognized it instantly – it was the same one Bennett and

Nelsonhad been swimming towards. Rick Savage smiled. It was one of the more distinct islands in the chain; an animal refuge, which made it an interesting choice as an escape route for the two friends.

Powerful kicks moved him closer to the shore. He watched as Austin, Ramirez, and two other members of his team rose from the sea, and ran across the beach. The men were two of his best; there was no doubt that they would catch Bennett and Nelson, but he wanted to be there when they did.

*　*　*　*　*

Moments later he pulled himself onto the sand and grabbed the water-resistant radio from his belt. "Savage calling Master Key. You there Jenkins?"

There was no squawk. No static. He looked at the radio in his hand.

A bullet had cleaved a path through its casing. Plastic shattered in his hands as he growled his frustration. The remains of the radio embedded in the sand as he threw the broken device to the ground. Shards of black landed in the depression of a footprint.

His own footprints tore at the beach's serenity as he raced to catch his men. There was no doubt they had radioed the situation to Master Key. But Baxter would want to talk.

Despite the urgency, he smiled; the thought of Nelson with his head in a lion's mouth made him happy.

*　*　*　*　*

"Okay, it smells funny," Steve whispered as he forced the brush out of his way.

"I told you." Paul kept a watchful eye over his shoulder. He was certain that they were being followed, and was the one who insisted on the whispering; but he had not given up on complaining about the island.

Designed as one of the premier tourist attractions in ImagiNation, the wildlife refuge was one of the first completed islands. Its vast topography and exceptional species list was the center spread of the first several brochures, PR releases, and online campaigns for the resort. It was here on Kingdom Key that residents and tourists alike could safari with all the adventure and little of the danger of a trip to the African savannah.

Kingdom Key's ecosystem was modeled after that of the Ngorongoro Crater: rhinos, elephants, lions, hyenas, and leopards roamed the grounds.

From the perspective of the guest, the ecosystem was seamless. The species intertwined in the precious circle of life and nature was free to run its course.

In reality, the predator species were separated from their prey by large ravines. These waterways were designed to maintain the illusion of the crater's functioning ecosystem, without having to replace countless zebra every few months.

"Down here." Paul scurried over the edge of a ravine and landed knee deep in the saltwater moat. "I am so sick of being wet. Next time, you're going to buy a condo in the damn desert."

Steve dropped in behind him; he felt no resistance from the current in the water, but the mud beneath him did its best to hold his feet in place. "What's with the moat?"

"Maybe this is where that guy built his castle." Paul lifted his feet high with each step to escape the suction of the muddy soil.

"Good. Let's raise the drawbridge and call for help."

"That's stupid, Steve. Castles don't have phones."

17

She had seen its conceptual art and had witnessed its construction, but every time Katherine entered the Amber Room, she was stricken speechless by its beauty. The semi-transparent sheets of amber were layered over mirrors and gilded scrollwork. The craftsman had created a masterpiece of luxury that made the entire room warm and inviting.

Usually the air was filled with the fragrant scent of the polish that was used to enhance the sheen of the amber. Now that was lost to the lavish aroma of the fine food and wine that filled the trays of the waitstaff.

White formal attire distinguished ImagiNation's employees from the guests who had chosen the standard black tie uniform for the evening.

The majority of the guests were accustomed to having the finest of luxuries served to them on silver platters, yet they still mused over the quality of the food as they plucked the hors d'oeuvres from their elaborate presentations.

Baxter had searched the world for the finest chefs, personally sampling their fare, and hired them away at great expense. He stole the head chef from the ranks of the French Laundry in Napa. Baxter had risen from his table, invaded the kitchen and hired the man on the spot.

Fresh ingredients were flown in daily by floatplane and prepared for the evening meal. And this attention to freshness was lost on no one in the room. Investors did their best to maintain their dignity as they shoveled food into their mouths. The representatives made no such attempt, as they stalked the bearers of the silver trays.

Katherine found a dainty and delicious bacon-wrapped mignon. Answering the call from her stomach, she wolfed it down. Then, answering the call from her nerves, she made her way to the bar.

"Ms. Bernelli." The bartender greeted her, "May I get you a water or cranberry juice perhaps?"

"Gin."

The bartender raised an eyebrow.

"Just pour." She thought of Paul and Steve and prayed that they were all right.

Antoine fixed the drink with a set of ice cubes and handed it to her.

She knocked it back and grimaced at the sharpness of the booze. A wave of warm calm flowed through her. She handed the glass back to him. "Now I'll take that water."

Water in hand, she turned to survey the room. No one looked bored or as if they had questions. They looked as if they had never eaten before, and as if each had forgotten their finer upbringings.

A guest, a rich man's aide, placed his hands on the bar next to her.

"Another please, Antoine." He turned to Katherine, "Can you believe this place? The food? The view?"

She forced a smile, "It is quite amazing."

"My name is Vincent Carlito. Vinnie." He extended his hand.

"Katherine Bernelli." She shook it.

"You know I almost didn't get to make it. My boss was dead set on coming down here. But a last-minute meeting in Denver dropped me on the boat instead. Thank God for that meeting in Denver."

Over the course of the last few years Katherine had come to despise the investor's representatives more than the investors themselves. They often spoke from a power they craved instead of one they possessed. But this man seemed sincere. His top button was undone and he leaned against the bar on his elbows, nursing what was obviously one of several beers.

"I'll tell you, this is probably the smartest investment he has ever made. This place is going to make a fortune. And I haven't even seen the other islands up close yet? Have you?"

"Yes, Mr. Carlito."

"Uh oh. You just got formal with me," he studied her up and down, lingering on the middle. "You work here don't you?"

"Yes. I work in Investor Relations."

"So, you're supposed to answer all my questions? Keep me interested so I'll go back and tell my boss to keep sending his money down here?"

She nodded.

"Well. You've got it easy tonight. I'm sold. I can't wait to see the rest of it all. I hear that you even have a zoo here?"

"Of a sorts. There is an island preserve modeled after the Ngorongoro Crater."

Vinnie Carlito tried to repeat the words after Katherine, but lost the pronunciation in his drink.

"The Ngorongoro Crater...it's in Tanzania."

"Lions, and tigers, and bears, oh my?"

"Lions, yes. But no tigers or bears. The designers tried to keep the island as close to the actual park as possible."

"Amazing."

"You must be excited to see the presentation. It should begin shortly."

"Another presentation. This Baxter fellow likes putting on the show, doesn't he?"

"The islands are his dream come true. He gushes about them as if they were his children."

"Children? Now that you mention it." He swung his arm wide across the crowd, "Where are the kids? This place would be great for families."

Katherine had not considered this before but shrugged the comment off. "This event is for the shareholders and their representatives only."

"Hrmph. My kids would have loved coming here."

The quartet grew still as the massive amber doors opened. Warren Baxter's smile competed with the sheen of the walls and could be seen from across the great ballroom.

He shook hands and lavished thanks as he crossed the room; he made sure to greet everyone who crossed his path. It was five minutes before he reached the dais.

"Here we go again," Vinnie said and ordered two more beers. "Ms. Bernelli. Can I get you anything?"

Lost in her thoughts, Katherine shook her head and smiled. "No thank you, I'm working Mr. Carlito."

Vinnie blushed. "Of course, I wasn't thinking."

"Listen, please don't tell Mr. Show-and-Tell what I said. If it got back to my boss...well, like I said, I have kids."

"It's our secret, Mr. Carlito. Please, enjoy the presentation."

Vincent Carlito tipped his beers to her and sauntered off to find a seat. Katherine turned back to the bar. "Give me another gin please Antoine."

"But, you're working."

"Just pour. You have no idea the day I've had."

Warren Baxter cleared his throat behind the microphone and beamed his smile in the general direction of the crowd, "Ladies and gentlemen... "

The amber panels on the grand doors crashed open.

Baxter stammered as men clad in black rushed into the room. Masks covered their faces. Each was armed. The group poured into the room, filed through the crowd, and covered all points of entry.

Gasps from the crowd were followed by screams as more men entered from the service entrance, leading the cooking staff in front of them.

The immense room was filled to capacity.

"What is the meaning of..." Baxter's defiant words were cut short by gunfire. Several of the intruders fired short bursts into the ceiling. One made his way to the dais.

Warren Baxter was roughed from his perch and thrown into the crowd. The figure in black said nothing. The rest of the force moved throughout the room and divided the crowd into two large groups.

Braver and drunker men in the crowd began to speak up, demanding answers, receiving blows to the head in reply. Most kept silent, complying with the gestures of the gun barrels. Rifle butts quickly silenced the dissention, and the groups were moved to separate sides of the room.

Katherine found herself in the smaller group, forced back, against the wall. The amber felt cold against her shoulders, and she was thankful that Antoine had already poured her that second gin.

She downed the drink. A hand on her elbow startled her. She turned to react but saw that it was Vinnie. He nodded slowly as he moved closer to her.

Silently, the intruders ushered the larger group from the room. No words were spoken. No demands given. Commands were delivered by the wave of a barrel. Katherine tried to look above the crowd in front of her.

Baxter was receiving especially terrible treatment. His hands were forced behind his head and the barrel of an assault rifle was placed in his back. His defiant voice surfaced again and he was driven to the ground. A knee was placed in his back and he was shoved to the ground.

Baxter grunted as he collapsed. A black-gloved fist dragged him back to his feet by his wispy strands of hair; he was forced through the amber-coated doors and into the hallway.

Katherine's group was led through the staff entrance. Compliance was immediate. Shuffling their feet, each prisoner trying not to kick the heel of the person in front of them, the crowd begrudgingly moved from the beauty of the Amber Room and into the unknown.

18

The water was briny and thick with the reclaimed dirt of the island. They slogged through the trench. Water rose and fell around them, ankle to waist.

Paul grimaced. "The smell is worse here. What is it?"

"Quiet," Steve concentrated on moving silently through the murky water. Rocks and an uneven creek bed made the passage difficult. His foot slipped off a rock and he fell chest first into the water. "I think this may be slowing us down."

"Look for a way out, then," said Paul. "This wasn't my idea."

Loosely packed sand formed the walls of the ditch. Thick grass was the only thing holding the top of the ridge in place. The walls had gotten consistently higher and steeper as they had moved on, and it had not been long before they had any choice but to keep moving forward. They had heard nothing behind them. The entire island was quiet.

They took no comfort in this.

The wind had carried the roar of an explosion to them earlier, but they could only guess what had happened. Either way, whether Savage had taken out the eco-terrorists, or vice versa, they did not feel entirely safe. Both groups had waved guns at them today; to root for either side seemed pointless.

One of the forces distracting the other was the best they could hope for.

They fought the mud and mire for fifty yards, through turns and twists, before they came to a rocky slope that afforded them enough of a grade to escape the trench. Steve gripped the loose dirt in his hands and pulled himself towards the top of the wall.

"Steve!" Paul's whisper was harsh. "Let me go first."

"Quiet."

"I'm armed."

"Give me the gun then."

Paul was going to argue but couldn't make a point. It would only cause unnecessary noise if Steve climbed back into the water to let him take the lead. He handed over the gun and tried to relax his fingers. They ached in protest at the absence of the weapon.

Bennett climbed. He tested the pressure of each foothold on the loose rocks, slipping many times as he inched higher. Within a few moments he crested the wall and peered through the grassy reeds at the top.

Then, just as cautiously, he lowered himself back down.

The astounded look on his face caused Paul concern. "Are they there?"

Steve shook his head in response. He did not even look at Paul.

"What?" Paul was getting impatient. If a man with a gun was not waiting at the top of the hill, why had his friend climbed back down? "What is it?"

Steve's voice belayed his disbelief. "It's a rhino."

"A what?"

"A rhino."

"What are you... ?"

"A rhino, Paul. Great big, gray with a horn that could pierce a truck."

Paul looked at the crest of the wall trying to imagine what his friend had seen. "That just doesn't make any sense."

Steve's face lit up, "We're on the wildlife preserve."

"The what?"

"It was in the brochure."

"I never read the brochure."

"Well you should have read it."

"Reading makes my lips tired."

"Well there were pictures." Steve snapped quietly. "And one of them was of a rhino."

"I'll read it when we get back, okay? Are we talking tigers here? Because the rule with tigers is never get out of the boat. And I am not getting back on the boat."

"No. I don't remember tigers. Lions, I think. Elephants, and, obviously, rhinos."

Paul looked at his empty hand. "Give me the gun."

"You're not going to shoot the rhino."

"I'm not going to shoot the rhino." Paul grabbed for the pistol.

"You'd just upset it."

"I'm not going to shoot the rhino."

Steve crept back up the top of the slope and peered over. He turned back to Paul and whispered down. "Do rhinos sleep standing up?"

"Let me check my field guide. I don't know? Do I look like Bindy friggin' Irwin?"

"I think they might be asleep."

"You're not thinking about tipping them, are you?"

Paul began to climb the hill. Soil fell from his footsteps and he slid several times before reaching the top. Steve was right; three rhinos stood twenty feet from the ravine.

"What are you thinking?" Paul asked.

"These ravines are probably to keep the animals separated. And I would much rather be in an exhibit with a sleeping rhino than with a prowling lion. Because, they're nocturnal right?"

"Why do you keep assuming I know stuff?"

"I have no idea. C'mon."

Steve pulled himself over the lip of the ravine and crouched low. Paul followed. Cautiously, they crept past the small crash of rhinos. Two lay on the ground. One stood silently.

Paul studied the large creatures before moving further. He was mostly positive that they were asleep, but his personal experiences with rhinos ended at the zoo. Faced with the situation now, he wasn't sure if they had been awake in the exhibits.

After a few moments he felt confident that they were asleep, and he started moving again.

They inched forward, each holding their breath as they took measured steps, hoping to avoid the snap of twigs or crackle of dried reeds.

Paul began to giggle when he realized that he was literally on his tip-toes. The absurdity of the situation had struck him as silly.

Steve turned with a scornful look and a finger to his lip. Paul shrugged, put his middle finger to his own lips, and held his breath again. When Steve turned back, the rhino had moved.

It swung its head slowly sideways; its black eye reflected the moonlight.

"Steve, rhinos do not sleep standing up."

The first burst of gunfire startled the rhinos. The second round put them on the defense. Their grunts were frightening and they turned frantically searching for the source of the disturbance.

The ground at Steve and Paul's feet erupted into plumes of dirt and grass. Paul spun to see four men across the ravine. Two were shooting. Two were heading for the lip of the chasm.

With assault rifles on their left and nature's tank on their right, Steve and Paul ran straight ahead. The rhino habitat was bare grasslands. No trees offered cover. No rocks. No shelter.

Bullets nipped at their heels and drove them on. A shallow impression afforded them the only cover in sight. Steve dove head first as Paul slid in behind him. The firing abated from across the gorge. Steve fired two quick shots at the crest of the ravine in an attempt to keep the two closest pursuers at bay.

"Still don't think they were going to kill us?" Paul tried to lie as flat as he could.

Paul watched the rhinos. The mammoth creatures had backed from the gunfire and taken up a defensive position within the small herd. They didn't seem interested in pursuing the two friends.

Steve tried to lie flat in the hole. It wasn't comfortable; between his wet clothes and the dry grass of the environment, he itched. The longer grass blades seemed to penetrate the shorts that sucked to his legs.

Shooting resumed and he tried to compress his body to the ground. The security force had taken aim again; rocks and dust fell over the lip of the depression.

"The two in the ravine will be coming soon," Paul had found a deeper portion of the hole and had a little more maneuverability than Steve.

Bennett grabbed a clump of grass that had begun to bruise his back and ripped it from the ground. It sparked a thought. He threw the clump at Paul.

"Grow up, would you? Now is not the time for a dirt fight."

"Paul, grab a bunch of these and tie them together with your belt." Steve struggled to reach into his front pocket. The soaked material clung to his leg, making it a challenge; moving his hand without getting shot was even more difficult.

Paul grabbed reeds by the handful and laid them across his belt. "How much?"

"All that will fit. Cinch it tight. You're going to throw it." Steve finally succeeded in wrestling the Zippo from his pocket.

"Here they come!" The firing had ceased to grant the guards in the ravine safe passage to the rhino enclosure.

Steve risked firing two more shots at the edge of the gorge. He dropped the gun and turned back to Paul. "Ready?"

Paul stuck out the tightly wrapped bundle of reeds. Steve flipped open the Zippo and spun the wheel. The faithful spark struck the wick and lit the flame. He held the lighter under the bundle and lit both ends. Dry grasses roared to life.

"Throw it!"

Paul stood and faced the slope of the ravine. The two guards were just beginning to pull their shoulders over its edge. Cinder scattered into the night as the flaming bundle soared across the plain. Paul dropped back into the relative safety of the depression.

"What're we hoping for with this? A wall of flames?"

"Flames, smoke, anything to give us a chance to get away." Steve watched the tinder bundle burn.

The roaring firebomb had landed just in front of the ravine's edge. One of the men caught a face full of embers and dropped back below the ledge. The other tried to knock the bushel into the water, but only succeeded in spreading the fire.

There wasn't a lot of grass by the edge but what was there caught quickly. Steve peered over the lip. He was sure the fire would slow down the two in the ravine but it wasn't enough to obscure them from the gunmen across the gorge.

He ducked as another barrage of bullets spat against the edge of the pair's hiding hole. He pressed hard with his weight to make himself as flat as possible. His ear mashed against the ground as bullet-flung rocks pelted his face. It was then that he noticed a low rumble.

The rumble grew into a roar. He pulled his ear from the ground and still it grew. The rhinos were charging.

Steve tensed his body, expecting them to run from the fire, down to the hole and over him and his friend. He pointed the gun in their direction knowing full well that a round from Paul's .45 would do no good.

But, the crash of rhinos did not appear. The rumble grew in intensity but not volume. Despite all sense, the rhinos charged into the fire. The three massive creatures beat their soles wherever the fire had spread. Smoke from the dying blaze mixed with dust and filled the air.

Steve looked back at the chaos and screamed to Paul, "Go! The rhinos are blocking the view."

Paul scurried out of the hole; Steve followed. The thunderous sound continued behind them.

They reached the other side of the paddock quickly and were greeted by another moat, but this one held the dry promise of a foot-bridge. Constructed of metal and as narrow as a man it was obvious that the rhinos could not use it as a means of escape.

Their footsteps rang the planks like a xylophone as they darted across the bridge. On the other side was a small compound of metal buildings. Several small sheds and a larger portable building defined the game wardens' offices.

Outside was a display featuring a map of the island; the Kingdom Key logo emblazoned across its center. The silhouette of a rhinoceros indicated where they had been. They had found the HQ at the center of the island.

Three golf carts were lined up to receive their nightly charge. Each was painted safari brown and mottled with black spots and mud.

They ran past the carts and crashed through the door to the main cabin.

The game wardens office was filled with little more than a desk and equipment lockers. Steve tried in vain to open the lockers. His hope was that they contained rifles, tranquilizer guns or something that could be used to combat their pursuers. Padlocks held firm against his excessive and futile rattling.

Paul appeared at his side and pulled the gun from his hand; two bullets sent sparks flying and tore the sliding lock from the frame. The door creaked open as the padlock fell to the ground.

Two flashlights, a first aid kit, and a shotgun were stowed neatly inside. A box of shells sat on the bottom of the steel locker. Steve fed rounds into the gun as Paul ran back outside to study the map.

"Where do we go?" Steve appeared beside him, pumped the slide of the gun, and chambered a slug.

The map display was massive and beautifully designed. Each section of the island was identified by its residents and information about the various flora and fauna that could be found there.

"North are lions. Zebras east."

"I vote, east."

"The dock is North." Paul ran his finger across the shadow of a boat.

"That's stupid."

"There's a path that takes us around the entire island, but I didn't think we had time for the complete tour.

"Fine. We go north."

* * * * *

Stale air filled the opulent banquet hall; its volume had been filled with the nervous breath of the hostages. They sat motionless. Several guards paced at the perimeter of the room. They cradled automatic weapons in their arms and stared intently out of the slits cut into the masks that covered their faces and hid their identity from the frightened prisoners.

The silence made the situation even more unbearable for the hostages. Whispers began more from frustration than as plans for escape.

The talk of terrorists was the first whisper that broke the hushed atmosphere. The group of armed men had remained silent and given no indication of their origin. Both their language and identities were a secret.

They were well-equipped. Every guard held a similar weapon.

Katherine didn't know what kind of gun it was, but with the stock tucked under their arm, it looked no longer than their forearm. Still, despite the small size, the weapon looked deadly in the arms of the mysterious men.

Pouches hung from straps woven into the black uniforms. The weight of their contents fought against the fabric. She assumed they held more bullets.

Expressionless faces hidden by fabric did less to frighten her than seeing the eyes of her captors. There was no emotion in the cold eyes. Each held the same gaze. Blue, brown, or gray, every eye held the same indifference.

She focused on the guard closest to her, and followed his stare. He looked above the crowd, his finger poised on the trigger guard of the odd-looking weapon, waiting to quash the first ill-conceived escape attempt.

The whispers continued.

"Terrorists, they have to be terrorists."

"Are they here to strike against America?"

"Are they holding us for ransom?"

"Some of the richest people in the country are here."

When she heard this, Katherine looked around the room and noticed for the first time that of all the millionaires and billionaires in attendance for the tour, not one was in the room with her. The crowd in the conference room consisted only of aides and island staff.

She looked closer at the faces around the room and spotted Brittany Hardy. The blonde was a fellow Investor Relations Specialist and had similar responsibilities. She was sobbing. She had tried to hide it at first, but it quickly grew to an open weep.

Katherine moved slowly. Not standing, scooting across the floor, trying not to draw attention to herself. She looked to Brittany, then to the guard. He watched. The dead gray eyes traced her movement.

She stopped. He did nothing. She moved closer to the weeping woman. It was soon obvious to her that the guard did not care. As long as she made no move for the door it seemed that the guard would not react.

Slowly she stood and with her eyes matching the guard's. She moved towards Brittany; the guard only watched. She reached the girl and embraced her.

Brittany jumped and glared at Katherine. It seemed as if she was about to scream.

"Brit. It's me. It's Katherine. Everything is going to be all right."

Brittany collapsed into her embrace, sobbing for a few more minutes before finally attempting to regain her composure. Katherine rocked her slowly and whispered reassurances.

"I'm so scared."

"It's okay, Brittany." Katherine cradled her head like a little sibling.

"What do they want?"

Katherine shook her head, "I don't know. But, they don't seem like they want to hurt us."

With a few short snuffles, Brittany stemmed the tears.

"Brit, are any of your investors here?"

Brittany looked at the crowd for the first time since the shots had been fired.

"No. I don't see any."

"Mine either."

"Not even that cute one?"

"What cute one?"

"I don't know. He was traveling with the new guy they told us about. Do you think he's okay?"

"Paul? Yes. I know that he wasn't here. He and his friend are with that jerk Savage."

Katherine identified several more aides and assistants.

"Brittany, where do you think they took them?"

"I don't know. I'm not even sure how we got here. It's all a blur."

A hand grasped her shoulder. Katherine gasped. Her blood turned cold, and she turned expecting to see the guard. But the grip was reassuring and gentle. She turned. Vinnie Carlito was smiling at her.

"Is everyone okay?"

"Fine, Mr. Carlito." Brittany answered.

"It's Vinnie." Carlito crossed his legs and made himself comfortable on the floor next to the girls. He surveyed the room. "My boss isn't going to like this aspect of the islands." The joke fell flat but he pushed it. "I may just have to advise Mr. Bennett to pull his money out of this dump."

Katherine gripped Brittany tighter.

"Mr. Bennett?"

"Yeah. He's got a lot of money in this place and I'm not sure that terrorists were in the brochure."

Katherine looked him in the eyes. "I didn't know you worked for Mr. Bennett."

"Yeah. It was a pretty nice deal up until now." Vincent Carlito turned to look at the guards.

Brittany chuckled despite the situation.

Katherine held her tighter and whispered in her ear, "We can't trust him."

* * * * *

The safari cart hummed to life and lurched north. Paul sat behind the wheel and Steve rode shotgun with an actual shotgun in his lap.

Tire-beaten trails radiated from the HQ. The northern path led them to an iron bridge that crossed yet another moat. This one was wider and deeper than the one they had followed into the rhino paddock.

Steel gates framed both ends of the bridge; steel mesh covered the sides and top. The thickness and solid construction of the caged bridge brought a chill to the two friends in the cart. Paul locked the brakes on the golf cart and stepped out to open the gate.

It didn't creak. It didn't moan. It opened on well-oiled hinges. This lack of sound caused the men to breathe a sigh of relief. The creatures beyond would not have been alerted to their presence. Steve opened the gates on the far end.

Paul leapt back in the cart and drove into the lion paddock. Steve closed the gate and got back into the cart. He lowered the gun and set it across his knee. The ratty vision of a dusty coach rider entered his mind. The weight of the gun on his lap gave him little reassurance. The fact that the dusty coach rider was always the first to die didn't help.

In his left hand he held one of the flashlights from the locker as a headlight. The cart bounced over the rough ground and jostled the occupants. Paul anticipated the turns and had a smoother ride; Steve was almost tossed out of the cart at every turn.

"Slow down."

Paul stomped on the brakes and lost control of the cart. It slid to a stop.

"Do you want to drive? Considering that just today I've been shot at, killed a man, been dumped in the ocean more times than I can count, and am now driving this thing by flashlight, I think I'm doing a pretty damn good job."

"I'm just saying slow down. I want to stay in the cart."

A roar floated across the darkness.

"Drive faster. Drive faster." Steve tightened his grip on the cart.

Paul brought the cart up to speed as Steve tried to determine the direction of the most frightening sound he had ever heard.

* * * * *

Water poured from the eyelets of his boots with every step, but Rick Savage wasn't worried about being quiet. He ran north along the beach. The shots had come from the interior of the island, and though he was confident that his men could handle the two guests, he decided to flank them should the annoying pair get lucky yet again.

Those fools on the barren island should never have fired on Bennett and the girl in the first place. But, once committed they should have just killed the pair and disposed of the bodies.

He was thankful that, after tonight, his ties with the group would be severed. They were unprofessional and gun-happy. Had they never fired, chances are that Steve and Katherine would have thought nothing of the group working on the unfinished island. They might never have even spotted them. Now there were two loose ends running around the archipelago and another back at Master Key.

He cursed the amateurs again and picked up speed. A quick swim across the channel had put him in the lion paddock. He gripped the Heckler and Koch USP tighter in his fist. He didn't know anything about lions aside from "king of the jungle" stories. But he wasn't taking any chances. It would be embarrassing to fall to a cat.

* * * * *

Austin hugged his injured hand close to his chest as Martin boosted him up to the still smoldering plateau. He winced as he tried to flex his fingers. He grimaced and groaned, "It's busted."

"What do you expect? A damn rhino stepped on it."

"Where's my gun?"

Sanchez handed him the twisted frame of the submachine gun. "It was at the bottom of the gorge."

Ramirez stepped from the ravine completing the four-man fire team.

Austin threw down the trampled weapon in disgust and reached across his right thigh to grab his sidearm. "I want to shoot them, now!"

"I think they ran straight to the middle of the island."

A snort brought their attention back to the massive animals only thirty yards away. The small crash of rhinos was now fully awake. Satisfied with their firefighting job, they had returned to grazing.

Austin eyed the massive beasts and then his busted hand. "Do you think they knew that would happen?"

Martin shrugged, "What are you whining about? You knew the risks when you took the job."

"I knew the risks and I am still willing to take them. But nowhere in the deal did it mention a possible maiming at the feet of a rhino."

"Get over it. The doc will fix you up when we get back. Just try to keep your whining down so you don't give us away." Ramirez led the team to the edge of the rhino paddock. Across the bridge they could see the lights in the game warden's shack. He signaled for the group to go low.

The unit reacted as one and dropped to their knees, each surveying a portion of the island's central hub. Seeing no movement, Ramirez led his team across the bridge and surrounded the shack.

Sanchez took point at the door. He stood to its side and pulled a metal cylinder from his vest. With one quick and practiced move he tossed the flash bang grenade inside.

The noise was sudden and devastating. Anyone in the shack would be instantly disoriented. The magnesium core of the grenade would activate all of the photo sensors in the victim's eyes at once, while the following bang would disrupt their inner ear causing enough disorientation for the team to move in.

Ramirez signaled the team to enter. The group swarmed the small steel building and found nothing.

"Spread out," Ramirez noted the grim look on Austin's face as he cradled his busted hand against his chest and led his line of site with the pistol.

The four men ran from the game warden's shed and into the yard of the hub.

Ramirez made note of the tourist map. Zebras east. Lions north. He studied it for a moment. Two possibilities lay in front of him. He would have to divide his men.

"Austin, Sanchez. You head east." They nodded and moved off towards the zebra area of the park.

"Martin. You and me. Into the lion's den."

19

Plastic shattered. Metal frames bent. The cart flipped over and crushed the canopy. Paul's reckless driving had taken them over a hill too fast. Steve was thrown from the cart and landed chest first on the shotgun. His sternum throbbed with a dull ache.

The cart had landed on the driver's side and Paul stood up from inside. "You okay?"

Steve stood and took note of his arms and shoulders. "I think so. But you broke the cart."

"I guess we run then."

"Okay, but run quiet. I still can't tell what direction that roar came from."

Paul scurried through the crushed canopy of the overturned cart and joined Steve in a quiet jog that pointed in the general direction they thought they should go.

"We'd better think of a backup plan in case there's no boat at the docks," Steve said.

"Of course there's a boat. There was one on the map."

Steve threw his friend a look that he had thrown him many times before.

Paul threw up his hands. "Look, I'm sick of swimming. I'm sick of being wet. My underwear has crawled so far up my ass that if I stuck out my tongue you could read the label my mommy sewed in there. I'm not saying I want to, but, if we have to, we can swim. The islands don't seem to be more than fifty yards apart on average. That much, even I can tell. In the dark. With no yardstick. Or concept of space."

Steve grunted his agreement. He had come to the islands to relax and maybe swim in the ocean a little. He had gotten his fill of swimming and the next vacation he took would not be to an island.

"I hope there aren't sharks." Paul said and focused on the rugged terrain in front of him.

* * * * *

Broken ground slowed Austin down. With every treacherous step, his hand ached and throbbed.

"Those rich kids are dead. Arrgh!" He screamed again as a depression beneath his foot sent a particularly large jolt through his body and into his hand.

"Quiet. You'll give away our position."

"What does it matter? We're on an island. Where are they gonna go?" Raising his voice, he continued the threat. "There's nowhere to go! You're on an island, you dumb rich bastard! We're going to catch you, and I'm going to kill you!"

"Shut up." Sanchez stepped towards his teammate, "Be professional."

"I am a professional. I've fought in countless conflicts with professional armies. I've taken out enemies in every climate. I've been shot, stabbed, knocked off my feet in an explosion, and even poisoned–once. But I've never had my hand stepped on by a fucking rhino. And it hurts! I want them to know that I'm coming for them."

"Fine. Now they know. But lions are attracted to sound. All right? They're inquisitive by nature and I don't think curiosity will kill them. So keep your voice down."

"This isn't the lion exhibit, retard. It's the zebra's. Ya' know little striped horses?"

"I'm not taking any chances."

"How do you know that about lions? Did you do work in Africa?"

"No, I saw it on Survivorman."

* * * * *

The dock was there. The boat was not. The map was wrong.

"It was a stupid map." Paul looked over the edge of the dock. Steve stood behind him on the beach looking across the channel.

"This looks a little farther than fifty yards."

"Sure. Who would want to live fifty yards from a lion? The smell alone would carry a hundred."

"We don't have any choice but to swim."

A whistle spun them around. Somehow, despite being sopping wet, Savage had snuck up behind them. His pistol was trained on Steve.

"Savage, it's us."

"Drop the shotgun, Bennett. And move out of the way. I want to shoot your friend first."

"What?" Steve held the gun tight.

"I told you he was trying to kill me." Paul said.

"What are you talking about? Put the gun away, Savage."

"Move Bennett." Even on the darkened beach, his rage was visible on his face. The scar on Savage's brow pulsed red.

Paul grabbed Steve by the shoulder and stepped behind him.

"Kill Steve first, he's got all the money."

"You're a coward, Nelson!" Savage stepped closer.

Savage raised the handgun and pointed it at Steve. "This is your last warning, rich kid."

Steve felt the barrel of a gun press into his back. He dropped to the ground.

* * * * *

The shots came from the northern path. Austin increased his steady gait to a full sprint and left Sanchez behind.

His hand ached with every pounding step, but the anger that burned in him was more than enough to block out the pain. He wanted to shoot the rich kid and his friend himself, but if the other team had reached them first he might not get the chance.

He screamed as he ran. Half at the pain and half at the frustration that he may not be the one to make the fatal trigger pull.

Ramirez was a good man and a fair poker player. Austin almost considered him a friend amongst the other people on the team. He thought that Ramirez may hold the pair so that Austin could have his revenge; but he couldn't be sure.

Another roar sounded. This seemed closer than the last. Austin remembered the map and kept running. The lions were across the ravine.

The map was wrong. It had, along with many other of the elements in the park's gift shop, been created by one of Warren Baxter's promising young nieces. She had always loved animals and was studying design in college. It was a gorgeous map of the park. She had minded the color palette and consulted with the printer on specs and formatting. But, somehow, the difference between zebras and lions had escaped her novice design skills. She had switched the two species' habitats.

The massive beast leapt from ten feet behind its prey and landed with its forepaws on Austin's back. Collapsing the man beneath its tremendous weight, the hunter locked into the man's shoulders and extended its rear claws. The lion began to work its massive legs, stripping flesh and muscle from the bone.

The screams reached Sanchez's ears just as he came across his teammate. He had not seen the predator strike and, despite what contempt he held for Austin, he pitied the man. The gun jumped in his hand as he fired quick bursts at the cat.

The first burst was an attempt to scare the creature off, but it did not deter the giant cat. As the monster's reflective eyes narrowed, Sanchez pulled the trigger. Over and over the bullets barked from the barrel. All training had left him, and he continued to pull the trigger well after the gun was empty and long after the lion was dead.

When it finally processed in his mind that the beast was no longer a threat, Sanchez rushed to Austin's side. The back of his ribs, broken and bent, was visible through the nylon vest. Pieces of him were strewn as far as fifteen feet away. He continued to scream and sob. Gasping with torn lungs, "help me," wheezed from his broken mouth.

Sanchez reloaded his weapon and helped him the only way he knew he could.

* * * * *

The sand was still warm from the heat of the day and it cushioned Steve's landing on the beach.

Paul fired. The slide of the XD locked open. It had been the final shot, but it had been enough. The bullet struck Savage in the shoulder. The slug dug into the flesh of the security chief's right arm.

Rick Savage was stunned. He screamed. Despite the lead in his arm he raised the gun to fire.

The report from Steve's shotgun made a mockery of Paul's .45. The shot struck Rick Savage square in the chest and took him off of his feet.

His head crashed against a rock that had been harvested, shipped and strategically placed on the shore of the man-made island, for aesthetic purposes only. Richard Savage lay motionless in the sand.

Steve jumped back to his feet, "What the hell was that?"

"What?"

"You put a gun in my back!"

"I had to let you know that I was going to shoot."

"You're an asshole."

"I couldn't exactly whisper it to you."

"Warn me next time."

"How?"

"Just..."

"Fine! Next time we're on a island paradise and some psycho with a glowing forehead has a gun on you, and I'm going to shoot him, but you're in the way, I'll ask you nicely to duck so you don't get hit by the bullet that's going to save your life!"

Steve stared at his friend for only a moment, "It's not easy being your friend."

"Yeah, but it's so worth it."

Steve pointed the game warden's shotgun at the lifeless figure. "Grab his gun."

Paul scrambled to his side and examined the man.

"It worked though. He's done. Look." Paul raised Savage's arm and released it. It fell limp to the man's side. He did it again and again.

"Knock it off. There are still more of them coming."

Paul left the body and walked back down to the dock. He checked the gun and found that the ammo did not match his.

He tucked the XD back inside the concealed holster and Savage's H&K USP inside his waistband. Steve slung the shotgun over his shoulder.

"Why do you think he tried to kill us?" Paul asked.

"We can figure that out later. Ready for another swim?"

"Ready."

Steve ran across the beach, dove into the warm water, and kicked to surface.

Paul ran across the beach and prepared to dive in when the USP fell from his waist. It hit the ground in front of his foot and was stuck into the surf.

"Hold on," Paul scrambled into the shallow water and peered in the surf. "Just a second." He felt around in the sand. Steve tread water while he waited for his friend.

"I think I've got it." He pulled his hand from the water. "Nope, that's a rock, shit."

After a few more rocks and a lot more swearing Paul found the gun. He rushed into the water and swam with the gun in his hand.

The two friends began the one hundred and fifty-yard swim to the neighboring island, praying that they would finally find a boat.

*   *   *   *   *

Brittany had finally stopped sobbing. After being in the room for an hour, it was becoming clear that they were in no immediate danger. They had received no orders, no threats. The men clad in black had said nothing.

Katherine sat with Brittany. Vinnie had refused the subtle suggestions that he leave. He was a question in her mind. While she tried to imagine the faces behind the masks, why this was happening, what could the terrorists want, her thoughts always came back to who this man, Carlito, really was.

It had occurred to her that she could simply ask him – call his bluff. But she hesitated, worried. Was he a part of the group that now held them hostage, planted in the group to quash attempts to call for help? Was he a competitor of Bennett's? Or was he simply a dumb reporter trying to get a scoop on the true story of the islands, a few snapshots of the rich and powerful in Speedos and bikinis?

She wasn't willing to take a chance just yet.

Nothing had happened since they were seated in the conference room. The guard simply stood over them with that menacing weapon. At one point another man in black had addressed him. Quietly. Whispering.

Katherine had strained to hear. Even a language would give her some clue as to who they may be. But the words were hushed and mumbled behind distance and fabric.

When her focus on Carlito's purpose did ease, she found herself worrying about Steve and Paul. She had seen them leave with Savage, and no matter what she thought of the security chief as a person, she knew that he was more than capable with a gun.

Yes, they would be fine. The other hostages were in more danger. If she was right, everyone in the other group was a major stakeholder in the island chain. Which meant they were rich, and would no doubt be ransomed or threatened into parting with some sort of valuable information or industry secrets. She wondered where they had been taken and how they were being treated.

* * * * *

Steve dragged himself onto the shore; Paul was close behind him. Both were exhausted. Never one for exercise, sports, or doing stuff, Steve's physical fitness routine consisted of an occasional hike or canoe trip. Even then, the canoe trip was more about drinking than paddling.

Paul didn't fare much better. No friend of the treadmill, he preferred exercising his elbow to breaking a sweat. They looked at each other, and it was clear that they would have to find a place to hold up and rest. There was little doubt to the two of them that they had left a clear trail. The other islands bordering the reserve weren't within swimming distance and sand did little to hide their footprints.

"I've got nothing left. We have to find a shady spot and rest." Steve did his best to dry the shotgun. He pointed the barrel at the ground and watched the seawater trail out. He had no idea what the saltwater would do to the weapon; he imagined that it wouldn't be good.

Paul nodded his agreement. "Maybe this parcel of paradise has something on it. Even if we could crawl into an attic or something. Just to give our legs a break."

"C'mon. There were at least four after us, not including Savage. We can't give up our lead now."

They helped one another to their feet and stumbled up another beachhead, to another tree line, on another beautiful island.

20

Martin and Ramirez slowed their pace. The lion's roar had startled them, and they had changed to a more defensive position.

Circling back to back, they stepped slowly over the dried earth of the artificial savannah. They watched the tall reeds over their gun barrels, each imagining the horrific carnage a lion could inflict.

Movement caught Martin's eye and he squeezed off a shot into the thick grasses. The report startled the hidden creature and it darted from its cover deeper into the reserve.

Martin watched the creature run. Black and white stripes made clear the error of the map.

The pair dropped their guard and quickened their pace towards the dock.

Sanchez had arrived moments before and was crouched beside the security chief. "We're going to need a clean up team."

"Is he dead?" Ramirez kneeled next to his fallen commander.

"No, but Austin is."

"Bennett and his friend?"

"Lion. We never saw Bennett."

Ramirez pulled the radio from his belt and tried again to radio for help. "Master Key?"

The radio was silent.

"Master Key?" Ramirez's vision clouded red as he thought about Austin. He didn't really like the man. He had been short-tempered and overly confident; the product of too many back issues of Soldier of Fortune magazines.

But, like him or not, he'd been part of his detachment, and Savage was going to be more than upset. If the man ever woke up.

His radio crackled to life.

"Master Key?"

"Master Key." The voice was winded and worn.

"This is Ramirez. Savage is down and Austin is dead. We need the doc to the preserve, now."

"Just bring him back on the boat."

"The boat is gone. Send him over."

"We're a little busy ourselves. We're in the middle of a hostage situation. We'll send a boat. Just get back here."

"Bennett and Nelson are still...," Ramirez was interrupted.

"They can wait. So can Austin. You're needed here. How bad is Savage?"

"Unconscious."

The radio was silent for a moment. "Bring him to, and bring him here. We need all the help we can get." The static cut and the radio went silent.

"He's coming around."

Sanchez helped the security chief sit up. His glazed eyes took a moment to focus.

"Where are they?" Savage tried to stand but found his legs shaky. Ramirez helped him back down.

"We never saw them. Best we can figure is that they swam for another island."

Savage studied his men's faces, and noticed one missing. "Where's Austin? Did he make it off the boat?"

"A lion got him."

"What?" Savage reached for his radio and found it missing.

"Boat's on the way, sir," Martin said.

"We're to call off the search. They need us back at the hotel." Ramirez forced the radio back into its holster.

"Under whose orders?"

"Michaels'. He sounded scared."

"He's always scared." Savage glared at his second in command.

Ramirez could see that Savage wanted blood. "Bennett and Nelson won't get anywhere. Even if they manage to get to the edge of the islands it's a seventy click swim back to Key West. All the long-range boats are at Master Key. Tomorrow we can flood the islands with teams."

Savage felt the knot on his head and grit his teeth. Blood ran down his arm; beneath his Kevlar vest, his entire chest ached. He was going to enjoy murdering Paul Nelson and, to a lesser extent, Steve Bennett.

* * * * *

It was a castle. Cold and domineering, it filled the landscape of the island. The walls were tall and real. Steve checked, believing it to be a fiberglass shell detailed to look like old rock. But the rock was genuine.

They crossed under a portcullis and into a courtyard.

Steve was lost in the scale of a topiary garden when he heard a slam.

Paul had found the release for the gate and was apologizing for the noise.

They both returned to the portcullis to examine the gate. It seemed strong. Again, it wasn't a fiberglass reproduction, but an actual castle gate, built of timber and iron.

It was the safest they had both felt in a while.

They made their way through the courtyard to the main structure. The door was unlocked – in fact it was missing a handle entirely. They crept inside the moonlit room.

Scaffolds lined the giant walls, drop cloths covered the granite floors, and tools were stacked with care. Though incomplete, it was obvious that inside was where the authentic reproduction ended.

Network cables and speaker wire hung from contact points in the ceiling and near the floor where jacks would be placed. It was well past midnight and there were no workers present. This spurred a thought in Steve's mind.

"I haven't seen anyone working on these islands."

"So." Paul moved to the archway at the end of the room. Steve followed.

"It just seems odd, that with so much construction going on, that we haven't seen anyone around."

"Baxie probably didn't want the collar colors mixing on his final big sell."

"Maybe. But, it still seems odd."

Moonlight passed through unfinished plate glass windows and lit their way as they moved from room to room. They found drop cloths covering expensive flooring in each one. Some rooms were decked in wood paneling; in others the paint was already dry, and the artistry of the texturing caused the men to pause.

"This is the kind of place you need, Steve. Unabashedly expensive."

"My place is fine."

"Your place is small. I told you before you needed to get a nicer place."

"What does it matter? I've been living out of hotel rooms in Toronto and New York for the past six months."

"Yeah, and the only reason those were nice places is because Campbell set them up."

"I'm not having this argument now."

"You never want to have this argument. I want to have this argument. You're rich and you need a new place and a new car."

"I bought a new car!"

"You bought a Chrysler. You need an Aston Martin. You need a Ferrari. You need a Porsche."

Steve withdrew from the conversation.

"I'm sorry. I wasn't thinking."

"Why start now, Paul?"

"I'm just saying. He left the money to you. Not so you could mope about it. Maybe he felt guilty. Maybe it was a selfish way for his name to live on. It doesn't matter. It's yours and it's what he wanted."

"And look where it's gotten me. I'm stuck in a castle on an island being chased by, who knows how many killers. And on top of it all I have to listen to you tell me how to be happy. It's not what I want. Maybe it would be best if I gave it all up."

"Slow down. Let's not talk crazy."

"Or, why don't I give it to you?"

"No." Paul did not hesitate, and when he spoke there was no snide tone in his voice. "Steve, I already have your money. I've probably spent more of it than you have."

"Then what do you want from me, Paul?"

"I want my friend back. You've been mostly mopey since you found out that – one, you had a father, and, two, that he was dead. I understand grief. I know that there are some things that may take some getting used to. But, and I mean this in all sincerity, money can buy happiness."

"Look at this watch." Paul held out his hand. "I don't need it. And, to be honest, sometimes I don't understand it. The little bulb in the middle confuses me. But, damn it, it's just so shiny."

Steve said nothing for a moment. He stared at his friend. And, then, at the watch.

"It is a nice watch. Did I buy that for you?"

"Yes, thank you."

"What are friends for, right?"

"Interest free loans."

Paul smiled and Steve chuckled.

"What do you want, Steve?"

Steve grabbed Paul's wrist and looked at the watch. "It's late. I want to get back to the hotel, make sure everyone is okay, rat out Savage, then I want to get to sleep."

"Okay, but let's grab a drink before bed."

"You're on. And you forgot to set your watch forward."

They crossed into the next room; a room that would one day be the study. Built-in hardwood bookcases lined every foot of the walls. One large window let the moonlight in. Blue-green shadows filled the room.

"It looks like a dead end." Steve turned to leave.

"Wait, hit the lighter."

Steve spun the wheel and the yellow flame fought against the shadows.

"Over by the back wall. It looks like a door."

They moved to the back of the room. The shelving had appeared seamless in the dark, but along the back wall an entire section of bookcase was missing. And, where the shelves weren't, there was a doorway.

Paul stuck his head into the doorway and saw a staircase. "The Count seems to be putting in secret doors. Oh, this place is so cool."

Steve took the lead with the Zippo and descended the stairs. A thump filled the narrow staircase. Steve whirled around to see Paul with his hand on a lever.

"Found the door. This should at least give us a place to rest."

Steve shook his head and continued down the stairs. They wound senselessly, seemingly taking them nowhere. They walked for a minute before they came to the bottom. The stairs had not led to another room, instead it had brought them to a narrow tunnel that seemed to grow brighter as they went on.

They came to a cross in the tunnel. The path to the left was in complete darkness. Moonlight awaited them on the right. As he moved closer to the source of the light Steve's Zippo flame began to dance and flicker in a breeze.

Paul felt the breeze on his face. "We're back outside. I think we should go back and wait out the night."

"Wait, we're not outside." Steve stepped from the narrow tunnel and into an open and damp room. "We're in the boathouse."

Paul followed his line of sight and saw it too. A channel had been dug from the island's coastline under the castle.

"Dude this is like the batcave. Who is this guy?"

Steve's eyes landed on the prize. Four jet-skis were tied up at the in-home dock; he turned to Paul. "Fire 'em up, Hot-Wire. We're going back to Master Key."

21

Captain Richards was awakened from a dream of his cabin in the mountains. As he shook the sleep from his tired eyes he began to think that maybe a condo would be smarter. His bones were tired. He could actually feel the exhaustion in his bones.

With a nod, he dismissed the ensign that had summoned him to the dredge's bridge as his eyes focused around the blur of dreams. He stood and wondered why he had been called. The weather was clear and he could tell from the movement of the deck under his feet that the engines were running properly.

The first decision he made, after he splashed water on his face, was to be very upset with whoever called him. But, as the desalinated water dripped through his beard, he shrugged it off.

"Go easy on them, captain. There's only one more round after this," he said to himself.

This voyage would deliver the second to last hopper of reclaimed earth from the Intracoastal Waterway. One more trip back and forth and he could hang up his cap for good. These two hoppers would top off the last island. His cutter suction dredge would be replaced by another in Wassaw sound that would pick up sand from the sea floor and deposit it as pristine beachfront property.

The captain strode from his cabin and approached the bridge. As he walked, he admired the ship. It was a good ship and a good crew. He would miss them as well. Aside from the boredom of an uneventful tenure, there was little to complain about.

He reached the foot of the stairs to the bridge.

"Captain."

Rogers, one of the crew, was standing on deck outside the superstructure. He waved the captain over and out into the night air.

Captain Richards followed the motions. Rogers disappeared around the corner. Richards stepped onto the deck and looked toward the bow of the ship. Three of the crew were examining the retracted cutter suction arm.

He approached the group.

"Is there a problem with the span?"

One of the crew sat astride the arm tying a knotted rope to the arm.

"No, sir. I'm just replacing one of the Jesus ropes. The old one was about finished."

Richards bit at his lip and felt the anger that he had shrugged off come rushing back.

"This is why you woke me? A safety rope?"

"No, sir," Rogers had reappeared behind him. "We need you to check the hopper."

Rogers and Carlson moved in on Captain Richards. They both grabbed him – one hand on his arm and the other on his chest.

The captain, still confused at the situation, struggled. He was much older than these men, but his footing was sure. Planting his feet against the deck he used the rocking of the boat to draw extra force into his legs. With a mighty shove he threw the men off balance.

The two crew members quickly found themselves against the rails.

Richards looked around desperately for a weapon. The only item he could reach was the worn Jesus rope the crewman had just untied. Its weight was substantial. Heavy knots on the rope served as a last grasp at life should a crewman fall overboard near the cutter's arms. The saying went that if they didn't grab the rope, only Jesus could save them. He hoped it could save him now. He knew he was fighting for his life.

The captain swung the end of the heavy rope as Rogers came at him. The final knot caught him in the face. Rogers screamed and threw himself to the ground, spitting teeth as he fell.

The knot had broken his jaw. Blood and teeth littered the deck of the dredge. Carlson came at the captain.

Richards swung the rope back to intercept him, but it was too heavy; without a long arc he could not force enough speed from the rope.

He felt the wind leave his chest and several ribs crack as Carlson drove his shoulder into his chest. The railing dug into the captain's back. He screamed in agony as he drew in a breath to replace the one he had lost.

Carlson was quick. He dropped to the ground and grabbed the captain's ankles, one in each hand. With one swift move he lifted the man off of his feet and swung him over the rail and into the full hopper.

Captain Richards did not struggle in the slurry. He couldn't. Earth and rock mixed with water – it was too thick to swim in, and too watery to stand on. Captain Richards sank quickly to the bottom of the hopper, drowning in the earth that he had helped reclaim.

* * * * *

The ride back to Master Key had jolted every last bit of energy out of him. Steve's arms burned from swimming and the cut on his leg still ached. Without hesitation, Steve vowed to get into better shape should he survive this vacation. Once he had rested.

They skirted the central island until they found the cove adjacent to their villa and beached the wave runners in sight of the hammock. The lights were on inside. After a quick discussion, they determined that neither could remember if they had left them on.

"It might have been me," Steve said as he let the water drip from his shorts. He was certain that neither his cell phone nor driver's license would ever work again. And despite the tropical climate, he found himself beginning to shiver.

"You never were very green, Steve. I told you to try harder."

"This from the man who throws out artificial Christmas trees."

"They are really hard to get back in the box. It's worse than folding a map."

"If I left the lights on, there's a good chance I left the back door unlocked."

"With my whiskey in there? What if someone broke in?"

Steve dropped to the ground and pulled Paul with him. One of the island's electric golf carts whirred up the path beyond the villa.

The cart passed without incident. The security guard at the wheel had looked bored.

"They don't seem to be looking for anyone. I think we'll be okay."

"Shouldn't we have flagged him down?" Paul asked.

"No, I want to talk to Baxter about this. I don't really trust Savage's little private army."

"Good point. But they're going to want to talk to us if we try walking into the party this wet."

Steve nodded at Paul and rose slowly to his feet. They ran, doubled-over to the villa's patio door, and stopped. They heard nothing. They saw nothing inside. Steve tried the door. It opened smoothly.

Again they waited and listened. They heard nothing but the hum of the kitchen appliances. They crept inside.

Steve moved toward his room. "Don't turn any other lights on. Change and meet back out here. If you want to talk to me come get me. Don't yell."

Paul strode into his own room. His luggage was still packed and on the bed. His suitcase was open and he tore into the largest of the cases. Inside a plastic case was what he was looking for – an extra mag for the XD. He pulled the gun from his waist, dropped the expended magazine, and drove the fresh one in. It was longer and held an additional three rounds of .45 ammo. He raked the slide and placed it on the bed.

He dumped a box of rounds onto the bed and began to fill the spent magazine. It wasn't easy. The spring of the new weapon was still stiff, and the skin on his fingers had become waterlogged and pruned. "I spent too much time in the tub."

* * * * *

Steve stripped. Every layer of clothing struggled to stay on his body. His undershirt stretched as he tugged on it, and he had to tear it off his chest. He could feel the grit of the sand grind against his skin.

His suitcase sat unpacked, and he stared at it, sitting there on the bed with the shotgun lying next to it. He moved to the closet where his garment bag was hung. The tux inside was a rental. On such short notice there was no way to get one made. Paul had taken care of it.

The dinner was a black tie affair and as he tried to brush the salt from his skin he thought it odd that he would now be dressing to the nines. They were running for their life, and to be on the safe side they had to dress the part of the super-spy simply to avoid attention.

He pulled the tux from the bag, but left the shoes on the hanger. Since prom, he had vowed never to wear rented shoes again unless bowling was involved.

He pulled a pair of highly polished Skechers from his suitcase. They were casual, but could pass for tux shoes as long as no one looked at them. They would be easier on his feet than the rental, and he figured that the rubber soles may come in handy.

His thoughts turned back to Savage. There was no way to tell if it was Savage alone, some of his men, or the entire security force that now had it out for him. Was he acting with the "environmentalists"? It was obvious to Steve that even eco-terrorists weren't this well trained or armed. It had to have something to do with his island, but he had no idea what it could be.

Steve looked back at the shotgun. He would talk with Baxter. But he wouldn't trust him.

22

More guards had entered the room where Katherine sat huddled with the other hostages. There were now two dozen total, each wearing the same black outfit and carrying the same menacing machine gun. The hostages had not been approached or spoken to since they were placed in the conference room. The guards had just stared through black eyes from behind the hoods.

But something had changed – they were now talking to each other. One of the new men leaned close to one of the original guards, murmuring softly. Katherine could not make out the words. With the masks covering their mouths she could not even read their lips.

The posted guard looked back at the hostages. He let his rifle sling to his side and approached them. He lifted his palms to indicate that they should stand.

The hostages hesitated. A shot rang out behind. Another guard had fired his pistol into the plaster ceiling. Debris filtered down. The guard fired a second shot, and the first guard gestured again.

The crowd rose on unsteady feet.

The commanding guard drew his rifle back. The other men in black moved in amongst the crowd and separated them into groups of four.

Vinnie held close to Katherine and Brittany, placing himself between the girls and the guards. Brittany gasped as one of the kidnappers approached their group. Vinnie reached back and grabbed her hand.

Once the groups of four were formed, the armed men began to lead them out the door. Vinnie Carlito tried to position himself, the girls, and another older man to be the last group out the door.

He offered a hand to the older gentlemen who was breathing heavily and looked to be in pain. It was an act of courtesy and concern, but at the same time it allowed Vinnie to stall, making his group as the last in line. The apprehension in the group had oddly waned over the last couple of hours. Now it returned.

Two guards escorted each group through the hotel.

Katherine wondered, like everyone, where they were going and what these men wanted. It was silly to try and stop the island project's progress now. All but one island was completely reclaimed. Did they seek revenge for what they saw as a crime against nature?

She found herself standing closer to Vinnie. His identity was still in question, but he seemed to have their best interests in mind.

Did he know Steve? Was it just a miscommunication? Steve and Paul had come at the last minute. Perhaps Vinnie did work for Steve.

No. She shook her head more confused than ever. His name was not in the file. She had memorized the guest list and the only surprises were Steve, Paul, and the terrorists that now led them down a dark hallway.

* * * * *

They walked the grounds trying to be as cautious and inconspicuous as possible while wearing elegant evening wear. Steve was already thankful for the Skechers. They hid the sound of his footsteps.

Paul touched the USP in his waistband to reassure himself it was still there. In addition to the gun, he'd pulled a full magazine from Savage's body, which he'd stowed in his jacket pocket.

Steve kept the smaller XD in his trouser pocket. Its size made it easy to slip in; its weight made it a challenge for the trousers' built-in belt. Steve found himself constantly adjusting, trying to compensate for the pistol's heft.

Bare paths and dim lights were all that met them on the walk to the hotel. They had seen no other guards since the ones by the villa. They heard no voices. They may have been responding to a call from Savage's men, but the lack of activity made little sense.

The hotel was well-lit and quiet. Steve and Paul stopped just across from the entrance. Steve pulled the itinerary from his jacket pocket.

"They should be in a place called the Amber Room. Some formal dinner." Steve said.

"And, undoubtedly another lecture from the King of Creativity."

"I'm sure we're on the guest list. We could just walk in."

"If you trust Baxter, but you don't."

Steve nodded, "We can't be sure he didn't order Savage to kill us. Any ideas?"

Paul thought for a moment and came up with nothing. "I'm all out of great ideas. I did the runaway boat thing, tackling you off the other boat, and sticking a gun in your back. Anything I think of now might get us hurt."

"I don't know what else to do. We have to talk to Baxter. If Savage was acting on his own, Warren shouldn't be upset that we killed him."

"You killed him. I just shot him."

"Either way, it shouldn't matter. He'll call in the cops and get it taken care of."

"Fine. So what's the plan?"

* * * * *

They approached the large doors of the Amber Room. Inside they could hear music. Steve pushed open the door. A sea of men in black ties and women in their finest gowns milled about the room. They were celebrating.

Steve scanned the crowd for Katherine. He couldn't find her but wouldn't be surprised if she had decided to skip the party and rest.

A hand landed on Steve's shoulder. His stomach knotted. Just walking in hadn't been the best idea. Bennett turned to face the man with the hand. Warren Baxter's grin was bigger than he had seen it all day. Steve could see his reflection in the old man's teeth.

"Steve, my boy! I'm so glad to see you here. You don't know how happy I am. I trust everything went well on the island."

Steve felt his muscles relax. He hadn't realized that he had quit breathing. He didn't figure that he would ever enjoy seeing the corny old man's smile. He sighed. "We need to talk, Mr. ..."

Warren stopped him with the wave of his finger.

"Warren," Steve continued.

"Absolutely. I'm thrilled you've joined us here tonight. You must have a million questions. But, I'm afraid our conversation must wait. I'm about to break the big news. The real name of this place."

"It's important."

"Not as important as this." Warren gestured to the podium. "I'm sure you have a ton of questions. Savage obviously didn't have time to fill you in on everything. We'll talk after I start the real party."

With this Warren Baxter sauntered off towards the podium. Ever the showman, he stood behind the mic and bellowed. "Ladies and Gentlemen. Welcome to our new nation."

"ImagiNation." Paul said mockingly.

"The Liberated States of America."

The room erupted in applause.

Steve and Paul spun to the face the podium in time to see a drape behind Baxter collapse to the ground. A large map behind him displayed the islands. They had seen the image a thousand times in the countless pieces of literature in the prospectus, on the web site, in their luxury hut. But, now, across the islands were the words that Warren Baxter had just spoken. The Liberated States of America.

"This is the eve of the birth of a nation. A great nation. A nation without poverty. Without crime. A nation built by all of us from the ground up. A nation created like no other to be the greatest nation in the world. The L.S.A."

"The L.S.A.?" Steve whispered.

"It does sound better than ImagiNation."

"What's going on?" Steve looked around again for Katherine. Did she know about this? Where was she?

Baxter continued. His genuine enthusiasm replaced the false grins he had been putting forward over the course of the day.

"The Liberated States of America is the realization of all our dreams; and tonight we are here to celebrate what we have accomplished – what we have built together. A perfect nation. A perfect world. An independent state that will grow on our ideals. A nation that will prosper without the burden of common men. What freedoms have been taken from us are now ours again. What restrictions have been imposed on us are now lifted. This is our country, ladies and gentlemen. And, we will only share it with those who we see fit. In one week we will secede from the Union. Remove ourselves from the United States and become one unto ourselves.

"Accountable to no one. Answering to no man. We will rule ourselves as we wish to be ruled. On your own island, there shall be only your law. It is your land. No one else's. But we shall share in the prosperity of the L.S.A. This paradise will better Disney World in attraction. The casinos will rival Las Vegas in the take. And we all shall share in the windfall."

The rhetoric went on. Baxter promised everything: peace, prosperity, security, leisure, and more. He didn't read from a teleprompter or deliver a rehearsed speech. He spoke with passion. It was frightening.

"Holy crap, Baxie is the evil mastermind behind this." Paul tried to whisper but was too stunned. The applause drowned out his words.

Steve could hardly speak. "I can't believe this."

"Actually, it makes sense. I mean he's got a giant map and everything."

"How could...?" Steve trailed off.

Steve had turned ashen. Paul put his hand on his friend's shoulder. "Steve, it's okay. It's not like you fell for this. You're not a part of it. It was your...oh, right."

Steve shrugged Paul's hand from his shoulder. "Let's try and find Katherine and get out of here."

They started to move through the crowd. Steve peered into the traitorous cliques, trying to spot Katherine's long dark hair.

Baxter was lost in his own fervor. The crowd wailed in approval as he struck the podium. Even with the microphone, Baxter had to shout to be heard over the cheers of the crowd.

The large doors to the Amber Room opened once more. Baxter didn't miss a beat. "And our island nation shall be secure. Thanks to our Secretary of Defense, General Richard Savage."

Steve and Paul crouched a half a foot each. They slowly rose to hide the conspicuous movement. They couldn't see Savage clearly. They did catch glimpses of the stringy dark hair and the crimson scar. It burned furiously as the man made his way to the stage.

Steve and Paul could not picture Savage saying anything they wanted to hear. They backed against the wall and began to look for a door. The crowd's pats and handshakes slowed Savage's movement; Baxter continued to praise the man.

Steve and Paul found a door and stumbled into a long hallway.

"You said he was dead!"

"I'm a drunk, Steve. Not a doctor. I thought he was dead. His arm kept doing that floppy thing."

They ran down the hallway and tried to put as many corners between themselves and the party as they could.

"What the hell vacation did you put us in?"

"Me? This wasn't my idea. It was Campbell's."

Steve stopped. Paul realized he was running alone and turned.

"What's wrong? Let's go. Killer behind us, remember?"

Steve spoke slowly and quietly. "Was this my dad's idea?"

"What?"

"This whole thing. Was he one of the founding fathers?"

"Steve, now is not the time."

"Was he a traitor?"

"No, he was a Canadian; so not a traitor. Look. I'm sure that not everyone who put a penny into this paradise was bent on starting a nation. Your father had to be one of the innocent ones. Right?"

"I don't know who my father was?"

"Daddy issues later, please. Armed men are trying to kill us. We have to find a way back to Key West."

Paul reached out, grabbed Steve's lapel, and tugged at him with his free hand. Steve snapped out of his daze and realized that Paul was holding the pistol. He dug into his own pocket for the

XD. Despite the streamlined gun, it caught on the fabric and he had to wrestle with two hands to get it out.

It finally came free from his pocket.

"Let's go."

They ran down the hall. It seemed to stretch on forever.

23

The Earth beneath his boots was mud. Plain and simple mud. Island 38 was the last island in the chain to be completed, and David Jefferson was certain it held the answers that he was looking for. The lynchpin that, when pulled, would collapse this abomination of wealth and greed.

They had watched it build. They had been there before the plans were approved. Before the deal was struck with Congress to allow its construction. The Rainbow Connection had set sail before the first dredge, and watched as hopper after hopper was dumped, sprayed, and raked into place to form the massive landmass. For years they stood by as nature was manipulated, shifted, and forced into the paradise built by Warren Baxter.

Baxter was a crooked man with a warped vision. His dominance over nature was just the most recent example of his use of power to get what he wanted.

The files were thick. The suspicions were damning and all this time there had been no proof of any misdoings. Jefferson now knew the man intimately. His background. His beliefs. But still the mystery eluded him.

"Sir," his musings were interrupted by one of his men. Dressed in black he would have been hard to see in the night without the aid of the night vision goggles. But, the brass casings in his hand were easy to identify. He pulled the goggles off and examined them. They were 9mm shells.

"There are plenty more on the western beach."

"Bag 'em up."

David turned pensively to the west wondering what would have caused them to open fire.

In the distance he saw the lights of a ship. Red and green lights on the vessel told him that it was approaching head on.

"What ship is that?"

One of his men answered. "The dredge. One more boatload of dirt. It should be here in about an hour."

David spat on the ground. "Then we don't have much time. Find it."

They worked frantically searching the bare earth. There was nothing on the island save for two Caterpillar bulldozers that were used to push the world around.

Twenty minutes later their search had turned up nothing and the men loaded back into the launch.

"Get in touch with the other teams. I want to know the status on Master Key."

The radio man went to work contacting the rest of the members. David looked long at the ship that was steaming towards them. There was only one scheduled dredge and dump after this.

They were running out of time.

* * * * *

Steve and Paul ran down the hall, twisting and turning through the corridors. Frustration built as they realized they were lost, but it included an odd sense of confidence that Savage would have a hard time following them. Baxter was certain to tell Savage of their presence. Savage would be certain to mention that they shot him. And the chase would be on.

Steve worked an escape plan over in his head. If Savage and Baxter were on the same page, then most, if not all, of the guards would be too. And since the Eco-nuts were also trying to shoot them for some reason, there was no one they could turn to for help. The phones were either out of service or never worked to begin with. Most of the boats in the harbor were sailing yachts or short-range craft. The ferry was not likely to pick them up this evening.

Escape seemed like a long shot. Paul led them around another corner and stopped. Steve ran into him and knocked him further around the corner. Paul turned and pushed Steve back, slapping at him as he shoved.

"What?"

Paul clasped a hand over Steve's mouth and forced him back against the wall. Steve was startled by the action and even more so that Paul was still holding his gun in the hand he had used to push Steve against the wall. His eyes went wide and Paul followed the stare back to the gun in his hand.

Paul lowered the gun and put a finger to his lips. He edged back to the corner and listened.

Steve crept behind him and strained to hear.

He could hear shuffling–like dozens of feet dragging. He laid down on the ground and poked his head slowly around the corner.

At the intersection of two hallways, he saw a large group of people being escorted at gunpoint. The groups moved slowly by and he began to withdraw his head when he saw Katherine. She was grouped with another beautiful woman and two men. One was younger and fit; the other was graying at the temples and had a serious stomach on him. Pit stains disappeared and reappeared with every sway of his arms. He was gripping his left arm and rubbing at it.

The guards weren't barking orders. As far as Steve could tell they weren't saying anything. They simply ushered the crowd down the hall. Katherine's group disappeared from view.

"It's her." Steve got to his feet and checked the indicator on his gun to ensure that there was a round chambered. A rocker switch was exposed on the top of the slide; it was loaded.

"Slow down." Paul sensed his urgency. "I saw men with guns. Big men. Big guns."

"There were three. Two with the group and a third pulling up the rear."

Paul chuckled at the word rear, but quickly regained his composure. "We can't go blazing in there."

"We have to do something."

"We don't even know what's going on."

"They've got to be Savage's men."

"Why would they take hostages? They've got a country to run. You don't even know if they've got an anthem yet."

"It doesn't make any sense."

"Well they'll need something to sing at ball games."

"The hostages, Paul." Steve was silent for a moment. "I guess not everyone was in on the whole L.S.A. thing."

Paul inched the slide back on Savage's gun slightly. The sheen of the brass on the round assured him that it was loaded. The hammer was down but experiments with the gun earlier told him that pulling the trigger would draw the hammer back.

"Still, why take the hostages?"

"Maybe to ransom for the right to secede?"

"Steve, Katherine's hot, but no one's that hot. Besides, the United States doesn't negotiate with terrorists. Harrison Ford said that."

"We've got to get her."

Paul shifted his weight and checked behind them. The hallway they had traveled was still clear. "Look, why don't we follow them for a while? Maybe there'll be a better opportunity to jump the guards."

Steve sighed and agreed. His temper raged at the sight of Katherine at gunpoint, but trying to attack the guards was suicide. He had only ever killed one person in his life. And apparently that person wasn't even dead.

Steve shook his head, "It scares me that you've become the sensible one."

Paul placed his hand on Steve's shoulder. "It scares me too."

Steve risked a quick glance around the corner. It was clear. He motioned for Paul to follow and they crept down the corridor.

* * * * *

The older man next to Katherine wheezed louder. She looked at him and for the first time noticed the grip he had on his left arm – he was having a heart attack. He began to breathe heavier, stroked his arm vigorously, groaned and collapsed. Katherine dropped to her knees in panic. She wanted to help the man but didn't know where to start. She ripped open his shirt. She had seen them do that on TV. That was as far as she got.

Brittany, the wreck of a hostage, snapped into action. Years of lifeguard duty and countless refreshers in Red Cross safety clicked in. She checked the man's pulse. There wasn't one. His breathing became shallow and stopped. She began compressions.

She weighed nothing; but her training gave her the weight to press on the man's chest.

The guards did not act to help save the man's life. They did not react at all. They kept their distance, but their attention was focused on the little girl pounding away at the dying man's chest.

Vinnie backed a step away from the group. The rest of the hostages and their captors had moved around another bend in the maze that was the convention center's corridors. Vinnie moved into the group that was gathered around the dying man.

Katherine didn't know what to do. Brittany was handling the compressions and the rescue breathing. She felt helpless; she stroked the older man's hair and whispered to him that it was going to be okay. The words were so slight that she didn't even hear herself speak them.

Brittany applied another series of breaths. She pinched the man's nose and locked her lips on his. She jumped as breath came back at her. Brittany pulled away and stopped the CPR.

The gray-templed man drew a breath and sputtered. The pain of breath showed on his face; cracked ribs from the compressions had already made themselves known. He groaned in agony, but agony meant life.

Katherine shed a tear of relief. Even the guards seemed to relax a little. Maybe they weren't intent on hurting anyone.

A shot blasted through the sense of relief, and a guard slammed against the wall.

Everything slowed. In a brief moment, no more than a fraction of second, Katherine's eyes darted to assess the situation. Vinnie was crouched next to the older man. In his hand was a short-barreled revolver. He had pulled it from his ankle, fired the shot, and then turned to his right.

Another round sounded; the report was amplified in the confined hallway. The guard that had been trailing the column grasped his shoulder as it erupted into a mess of blood and sinew. He fell to the ground and began to scream.

The remaining guard reacted. His reflexes drew the trigger and he started to fire before he could aim. Brittany and Katherine lunged back trying to avoid the stream of bullets.

Katherine cleared the stream. Brittany was grazed by a round. A streak of crimson quickly ran down the side of her calf. The heart attack victim was not so lucky. The fire from the submachine gun perforated his chest. He coughed briefly; dark red spittle sprayed from his lips as his lungs filled with blood. He was dead a moment later, and, this time, no amount of CPR would bring him back.

Vinnie continued his turn and fired three more shots. Three struck him back: one hit his hip, another his stomach. The third tore the gun from his hand.

Brittany screamed as the guard took careful aim at Vinnie. Suddenly, the guard arched his back, wrenching in pain. Two more reports sounded and he fell.

The first guard, who had been struck in the shoulder, regained his footing and his weapon just in time to also fall victim to a well-placed shot. He collapsed. Behind him, at the end of the hall, Steve Bennett and Paul Nelson crouched. Each held a gun.

Katherine smiled, the horror of the moment before was replaced with elation. "Steve."

"Stay down!"

Two guards had responded to the shootout.

Paul saw them first, and fired a quick round to the end of the hallway to keep them behind the corner.

"Come on!" Steve yelled over the sporadic fire.

Katherine grabbed Brittany by the arm and forced her towards the two friends. Brittany pulled her arm free and scrambled to the bleeding body of Vinnie Carlito. "Vinnie," She started to cry. It was obvious that he was dying.

He seized in pain and strained to talk. "Get to the rainbow." With a great deal of pain, he rolled onto his seeping stomach. Supporting himself with his right arm, he reached out with his left and grabbed the weapon off of the fallen guard.

Another shot sounded and the pursuing guards ducked back behind the shelter of the plastered wall.

"Go!" Vinnie screamed in agony as he pointed the gun down the hall.

Brittany hesitated.

"Britt," Katherine screamed and reached out for her hand.

Brittany lurched to her feet, and ran to Steve and Paul. Together the four ran from the firefight. The reports continued behind them; but only for a moment. The din of the shootout was replaced with the scramble of guards as Vincent Carlito collapsed.

24

Steve held Katherine by the wrist and kept the gun trained behind them. They ran back through the hallways. Steve knew it was only a matter of one more twist or one more turn before they came face to face with Savage and his crimson-anger eyebrow.

Paul was thinking the same thing. He and Brittany had taken the lead.

"In here." Paul grabbed for a stairwell door. The group darted inside and Paul closed the door quickly and quietly behind him.

The stairs led up. Only up. With weary legs driven by adrenaline, they climbed. The girls took the lead. The two friends stayed behind, both to cover their escape and to try and not look so tired.

"That's it. I'm getting a Stairmaster. I'm going to use it. And I will never be this tired again." Paul took the stairs two at a time but found his toes falling short of the ascent. He tripped. He managed to catch himself with his hands instead of landing on his chin, but the jar set off the gun.

The shot ricocheted around the cement stairwell. Everyone ducked. Everyone shrieked. The bullet bounced harmlessly back down toward the door.

Paul laid on the ground and looked at a divot in the floor mere inches from his face. "Yep, that should tell them where we went."

He leapt back to his feet. His face was now flush with exertion and embarrassment.

Paul noted the stenciled "6" on the concrete wall. "This place only has seven floors. And we're running out of them. Do you have any idea where we're headed?"

"The roof."

"Oh, man. I hope they've got a fire pole."

They reached the roof access door. Steve kicked it open and leveled the weapon. There were no guards on the roof.

There was a helicopter.

$* \quad * \quad * \quad * \quad *$

David sat and stared at the dash of the launch. He felt as the black shipped look. The riddled boat was slowly sinking. Jefferson was mired in the outcome of the raid. The men in the Zodiacs had found nothing on the lush island where they had retrieved their fallen friend.

His team had found nothing amid the mud on 38, still, everything cried out to David that Baxter was dirty; his henchman, Savage, was equally suspect. The chief of security had military records in every despicable army in the third world. He had sold his murderous skills to the better funded army in conflicts around the world; their cause didn't seem to matter. Savage had run guns, fired guns, and killed for every opportunist in any unstable nation. His presence here was no soft job; the gunfight had proven that.

They were protecting something, and once Savage dried off, if he wasn't dead, he would be coming for the Rainbow Connection.

Jefferson's forces were regrouping there now. The mission, the five-year mission, would have to be scrubbed. The best they could hope for was to still get out with their cover intact and hope that ImagiNation's shareholders still truly believed that they had been there to protect the coral. David spat over the launch's side as his radio man approached.

"Vinnie didn't check in sir."

David stared back.

"He missed his last two reports."

"Turn toward Master Key. I'm not losing another man."

* * * * *

"Okay, I'm getting a Stairmaster and helicopter pilot lessons." Paul moaned at the uselessness of the private helicopter before them. It was their salvation, if only one of them could fly it. None of them could. Steve had never even seen one up close.

They had barred the doors to the roof with potted palm trees. It had taken all four of them to move the towering plants, but they felt confident that it would buy them some time.

"The radio." Steve pointed back to the helicopter.
Paul threw open the door and jumped into the seat. He didn't even know whether it was the pilot's seat or not. The number of gauges, dials, levers, and buttons amazed him, but after a brief search, he was able to find the radio.

"What's the emergency channel? Anyone?"

Katherine told him. It had been a part of their training.

He quickly dialed it in and put the headset on. After a few moments he found the switch for the headset.

"Mayday, mayday... "

Steve slapped him on the shoulder. Paul looked at him, shocked. "What?"

"We're not in a sinking boat."

"It means 'come help me.' From venez m'aider. Fredrick Stanley "Big Johnson" Mockford coined the phrase in 1923."

Steve stared back at him. "You were searching Big Johnson on the internet, weren't you?"

"I was looking for a new nickname."

Steve blinked.

"S.O.S?" Paul asked.

Steve shrugged. Paul turned his attention back to the radio. "Help, fucking, help! We are being shot at – a lot – and we can't get off of this shitty island. We're in the retarded land of ImagiNation and people are trying to kill us. We are on Master Key... "

Gunfire cut him short. The palm tree held. But several shots had pierced the door and shattered the pot that held it fast.

"Get here quick. Over." Paul threw the headset off and hopped back to the ground.

Everyone in the group searched the roof looking for an escape.

It dawned on them both at the same time. "The statues."

They raced to the edge of the roof. The girls followed. Katherine looked over the edge and cringed at their obvious thought. "No."

* * * * *

Baxter's oratory concluded to thunderous applause. The new citizens celebrated as if this was their naturalization ceremony – their personal swearing in.

Baxter smiled, waved, and stepped down from the dais. Savage stood waiting impatiently. Baxter frowned. He could tell Savage was furious. The scar above his eye blared a deep red. He knew that this warning light had been the result of a serious head wound in the mercenary's past that left a scar whose skin was thinner than the surrounding area. When flushed with rage, the anger showed through.

"Your temper is showing, Savage." He spoke calmly while still smiling and acknowledging the adoration of members from the crowd.

"Bennett and Nelson escaped. One of my men was killed by a lion. Why did you call me back here?"

"What do you mean they escaped? They were just here, in this very room."

"Here?"

"I spoke with them. They were dressed for the prom."

"And you let them go?"

"They were here for the announcement. You spoke with them. They were here to become citizens." There was a defensive hint in Warren Baxter's voice.

The red scar on Savage's head intensified. "I never spoke to them."

Baxter stepped closer, turning his back to the crowd. He leaned in close, "I told you to explain the situation. I wanted Bennett on board. Now they know everything. What happened?"

"The damn hippies showed up and opened fire. The two boys slipped off the edge of the boat."

"Find them. They were here moments ago."

The applause in the room finally subsided. The room full of investors was still loud, but there was a faint burst of fire from deep inside the hotel.

Savage motioned to another security guard that was talking into his radio. The guard approached and spoke, "A group of the hostages escaped. They think it was Bennett and his friend."

Savage snatched the radio from the guard's hand. He pressed the talk button with such force that the impact resistant plastic cracked under the pressure.

"Follow them and wait for me. Understand? No one kills them but me." He slammed the radio into its case and barked at the guard. "Give me your weapon."

The guard cowered as he handed over his gun. Savage chambered a round and placed the gun in his holster. He started to leave, but, before he could join the pursuit, Baxter stopped him.

"I want them alive. The boy may need time to think this over. He just needs time."

"They shot me," Savage protested.

Warren Baxter sighed deeply. "I don't need Bennett. But his company would make the first months here much easier. Being a Canadian entity, they could not cry treason.

"Catch them and bring them to me. I'll talk to Bennett myself."

Savage held up the radio. "They killed my men."

"Do it. Rest assured that in a few months we won't need them at all. Then you can exact your revenge. For now they will be kept alive."

Before Savage could leave Baxter added, "And, please, take care of those damn hippies."

Savage stormed off to the far side of the room and flung open the door to the hallway.

Baxter watched as the pneumatic arms retracted the door. It closed, and the party continued.

25

The open spiraled columns rose the full seven stories of the hotel. The spires on top continued beyond the roofline. Baxter had surely said that they were symbolic of something or other, but right now they meant a chance to escape.

The columns were freestanding and a space of four feet separated them from the roofline. Katherine backed away from the building's edge. She was beginning to panic. Her breaths were coming faster and growing briefer. There was no other way off the roof, but this was not an option for her.

Steve saw the panic in her eyes and grabbed her by the shoulders. "Katherine? Katherine."

He could see that he was losing her. He leaned in and kissed her. Her breathing slowed, distracted by the kiss.

It lingered longer than he had expected; but he enjoyed it. He pulled his lips away from hers.

"I am terrified of heights."

He looked into her eyes and spoke softly. "If there was any other way we would take it. We have to do this."

She nodded; he could see that she was fighting the urge to lose control.

"The gap isn't that large. I'll go first. The open part in the middle is big enough for us to fit inside." He spoke slow, reassuring her with every word that it would be okay. "Paul will hold you until I have you. Once inside the column it will be a simple matter of lowering ourselves down."

She bit her lip and nodded again. He didn't know if she was agreeing or building up her confidence.

"You can do this."

She looked deep into his eyes and found the confidence she needed.

"There's a fire escape," Paul interrupted.

"What?"

"There's a fire escape. In the back."

Steve grabbed Katherine's hand and followed Paul to the rear edge of the roof and peered over. It wasn't a fire escape, but an access ladder. It was placed in a recess in the building and was painted to match the exterior. It blended in perfectly.

"I'll go first, you follow behind me."

Katherine agreed and Steve disappeared over the side. Paul took Katherine's hand and helped her over the edge of the building. He smiled at her and whispered. "I think he likes you."

Katherine cautiously followed Bennett down the ladder. Each step was preceded by a deep breath. The paint scheme on the ladder was so perfectly matched to the wall that she found herself descending by touch rather than by sight.

Each rung brought her closer to the ground and she focused only on reaching the safety of terra firma. She built a steady rhythm and found herself moving quickly, only slowing when she stepped on Steve's hand.

He didn't react, but it hurt.

She slowed her descent, quickly counting to three before lowering each foot to the next rung.

* * * * *

Back on the roof, Paul took Brittany by the hand. Her rescue attempt seemed to have eased the shock of the situation. Since grabbing her from the line of fire in the hallway, this was the first time Paul had really looked at her.

She was gorgeous. In addition to the training, she had also retained the body of a lifeguard. He noted that she wouldn't be doing any bay watching, but she was in perfect shape – even the wound on her leg couldn't slow her down. Her blonde hair draped slightly over her shoulders and she looked at him with green eyes that warmed his heart like a shot of Jack Daniels. For the ninth time since stepping off the plane in Florida that morning, Paul Nelson fell in love.

"I'm Paul."

"Brittany."

He took her hand and helped her up over the ledge. She placed her feet on the top rung of the ladder.

"Brittany. Do you like limericks?"

She smiled. Steve yelled. Paul gently let go of Brittany's hand and she started to climb down the ladder.

"This place is great." Paul smiled and threw his leg over the ledge.

* * * * *

Steve had reached the last ten feet of the ladder only to find it blocked by a panel of sheet metal padlocked over the ground level rungs. He told Katherine to hold. She had kept up her constant rhythm and had almost overtaken him a couple of times. Now that she had to wait, her fear began to build.

Steve let his legs dangle free and lowered himself rung by rung by hand until he was gripping the sheet metal. It was thin and it bit into his fingers. His six-foot figure put his feet a mere four feet from the ground. He let go and dropped.

Normally the impact would have been minimal, but his tired legs failed to absorb the shock. He lurched forward into the sheet metal panel with a bang and fell backwards.

He was able to roll and avoid hitting his head, but it still took him a moment to recover.

"Steve?"

"I'm okay. Lower yourself down and stand on my shoulders." He placed his back to the covered ladder.

Katherine took her time. She was hesitant to surrender her footing; once she did, she descended rapidly.

Her feet hit his shoulders solidly and hard. She wasn't heavy, but the momentum hurt.

He grabbed her ankles and guided her one leg at a time to place her knees on his shoulders. Her arms were stretched to the limit, and despite the pain in her fingers she refused to let go.

"I've got you. Let go."

She trusted him and took a breath. She closed her eyes and released her grip. Steve lowered her gently to the ground.

She opened her eyes to find herself in his arms. This time she kissed him.

"Thank you."

A steel door flew open fifty yards down the back of the building. The crash of the door broke the moment.

Paul shouted from above, "Steve! Run!"

Steve looked up to gauge his friend's progress. Paul wasn't on the ladder. He had leapt to a hotel room balcony, and was helping Brittany onto the landing.

Steve drew his gun and looked back to his friend. There was nothing he could do. To stand out in the open was suicide.

Paul kicked in the glass of the French doors to the hotel room and directed Brittany inside. He drew the USP he had taken from Savage and fired down on the emerging guards.

This gave Steve a single moment to run. He wanted desperately to stay. Safety in numbers aside, he didn't want to leave his friend. But, there was no choice.

"Steve!" Katherine ran and he followed closely behind her. The gunfire stopped and Steve risked a glance back to the balcony. Paul was gone; the guards were coming.

* * * * *

Paul made his way across the room, cracked the door open, and peered into the hallway. It was empty. They slipped out of the room, and followed the hallway to the elevator. There had been no eruption of gunfire from below, and the thought that his friend might have been captured tore Paul up.

"Come on," he said.

Brittany was right on his heels. He had to find a way to get back to Steve.

Steve didn't know it and Paul didn't show it, but the childhood friend hadn't been joking when he volunteered to be his head of security.

Steve had laughed and agreed. They had spent the rest of the evening drinking and discussing other nonsensical titles to justify Paul's outrageous salary.

Paul had hit the internet the next morning. He'd found a personal protection training academy in town, and while Steve dealt with the volumes of paperwork, Paul learned all he could about private security. He had gotten certified for his Texas concealed carry license. He learned how to shoot and how to recognize a threat.

His actions on the security boat were borne of his training. Other possibilities had not entered his mind. The tackle had been reflexive.

He had stayed with his bodyguard classes and had added martial arts to his schedule. He wasn't good at it, but he was improving. He always told Steve that he was out at the bars, and made sure to smell like whiskey when he met Steve after his classes. That part was easy.

He even convinced Steve that it would be fun to take an evasive driving course out in some desert. Paul paid close attention. This was serious even if it was fun driving a car 30 mph in reverse.

Steve was convinced that he didn't need security. He had always been too trusting. Paul had vowed to see to it that no one took advantage of his friend, and that no one would hurt him.

He had purchased the gun for muggers, would-be kidnappers, and those guys that drive the black van and grab rich folks off the street. He had seen the story on 60 Minutes. Sure it focused on South America but there were plenty of black vans in America, too. He had seen them.

Now here he was in over his head; and on top of that, he was separated from his charge and best friend.

He mashed the call button for the elevator. He had to get back to Steve.

"What about the rainbow?"

Paul shook his head as if he had been hit and looked at the beautiful woman standing beside him.

"Vinnie said, 'get to the rainbow' just before he died."

"Who the hell is Vinnie?"

"The hostage who had the gun."

"So who was he to talk about rainbows."

"I don't know. Katherine said we couldn't trust him."

"Why?"

"She mentioned it after he told us that he worked for someone named Bennett."

"I work for someone named Bennett." He gestured wildly back towards the room with the gun. "That was Steve Bennett."

"So you know him?"

"The only person that works for Steve Bennett on this island is me. And what the hell is a rainbow?"

Brittany shrugged. "That's what he said. He shot those kidnappers. I think he was trying to help us."

"The only thing I know about him for certain is that he is a liar. And I'm not searching for any rainbows. I have to get back to my friend and get us all off of this island."

The elevator arrived. Paul held the gun on the doors as they opened; the car was empty. They stepped inside and Paul hit the lobby/casino button.

Paul was even angrier now – an imposter, tree huggers with guns, crooked security, a whole new country. He screamed in frustration.

Brittany was silent for a few moments while the doors slid shut. Finally she spoke. "Paul?"

"Yes." He realized he was taking out his frustration on her, and she didn't deserve that, because she was hot.

"I do like limericks."

He turned and smiled at her. "I know a great one."

26

Savage had kicked open the rear door and had been the target of Paul's first shot. Pain ripped through his body when he threw himself out of harm's way and landed on his wounded arm.

He'd been shot before. He'd been shot more than once. He had been shot by professionals – soldiers, bodyguards, law enforcement; but never by a pretender like Paul Nelson. His chest ached from taking the deer slug in the vest, but his arm screamed in shame.

The firing had stopped and he kicked the door open again. The balcony was empty. Bennett and the girl were disappearing behind the corner of the hotel.

Savage sent four men after Nelson. Through gritted teeth, he reminded them that he must be taken alive. This is why he chose to pursue Bennett himself – if he caught Paul it would be all but impossible not to shoot him.

Two guards joined him as he set out after the overnight billionaire. He radioed the rest of the patrol. With the charade over and the L.S.A. partners enjoying their party, his men were now free to patrol Master Key. They were no longer a simple security force. They were a nation's military branch.

And, once Bennett was back under control, he would finally be able to deal with the ship of fools that had caused him so much grief for so long.

A squad was already heading to the armory. He glanced at his watch. They should be arriving about the same time as the dredge. That should make things more efficient.

He signaled his men and they followed Bennett and the girl.

* * * * *

Steve panted. He was certain now that he had never been so tired. His legs ached and he wondered how they still responded. He was slowing Katherine down and he could see it.

She was fit, thin, and had only been chased and shot at half as much as he had that day. She kept pace with him as she led the flight.

He recognized the path; she was taking them back to the boats. There was no other choice and he cursed the islands again. Into the water, out of the water, into the water, over, under, around and through the water. He felt as if he were drowning from his lack of options.

They reached the docks without encountering a patrol; Steve constantly looked over his shoulder. He blindly fired a round every time he caught a glimpse of their pursuers. It was often.

Savage chased but did not fire. The group of security guards closed quickly. Savage yelled after him.

"We just want to talk Steve."

They kept running. The docks were abandoned. The security boats were gone. Steve guessed that they were out dealing with the environmentalists.

Katherine ran ahead of him. Steve dropped to one knee and leveled the gun at the path. As soon as Savage stuck his head around the corner, Steve fired three quick shots.

Katherine all but dove into one of the jet-boats and fired the engine. She pulled alongside of Steve.

Two more shots kept their heads down, and Steve somehow found it in his legs to leap from the dock into the boat.

Katherine gunned the throttle and cut the wheel. She had no idea where to point the boat except away. The coast was too far. Even Fort Jefferson at Garden Key in the Dry Tortugas National Park could prove difficult to reach in the little jet-boat.

Their only chance was to get lost in the islands again. There were over four hundred. Surely they could find a safe place to hold up and think of a plan.

Steve landed hard on his feet and almost continued over the side. He dropped to his knees and stopped himself with his chest against the gunwale.

"Go," he wheezed trying to get air back in his lungs.

The bow of the boat planed out of the water, and pointed to safety. Steve peered over the stern to see Savage and his men sitting on the dock of the bay.

The crimson scar had finally faded and Steve thought he saw the man smile; it was a crooked grin that caught the moonlight and reflected a horrifying light.

The impact was sudden and, once again, Steve found himself in the water.

* * * * *

The hotel elevator reached ground level, and the doors opened. Green Day's Welcome to Paradise invaded the quiet casino. Paul peered around the door into the casino. It was impossible to see past a row of slot machines. Though the casino was void of gamblers or staff, the lights of the machines made it hard to detect any movement.

With a deep breath he stepped into the elevator lobby and waved for Brittany to follow.

"Where's the front door?"

She pointed and they began to run.

Shouts soon followed. Four guards had burst from the stairwell door. Paul fired three shots and hit a slot machine, a roulette wheel and the floor in front of him.

A burst of machine gun fire ripped back across the empty casino. Chips and cards flew into the air. The last few rounds chipped away at the ornate ceiling as the sergeant knocked the barrel into the air.

"Alive." The sergeant barked, letting go of the barrel.

Brittany and Paul dropped to the ground.

Paul whispered, "You lead the way."

Brittany started crawling. Paul froze as he watched her crawl toward the front door.

"Baxter is a nutcase but he sure can hire people," he said to himself and scrambled on all fours so he would not lose sight of the girl.

He enjoyed the view until they reached the lobby. Brittany stood and burst through the doors into the warm night air. The humidity hit her hard in face. The guard hit harder. She fell to her side, but caught herself on the spiral column.

As one guard ran to subdue the girl, a second swung at Paul as he came through the door.

Paul wasn't looking where he was going. He ran too close to the guard for the punch to be effective. The guard's arm wrapped around Paul's neck. The brute locked his arm and began to squeeze.

Paul gasped for air as his face was crushed against the guard's chest.

Brittany's attacker turned to assist with Paul.

The guard struck the gun from Paul's hand, "I've got him. Get her."

Brittany was back on her feet, a purple bruise already forming on her cheek. She struck at the guard. There wasn't much behind the punch, and if she had landed it she would have most likely snapped her own wrist; but it startled the guard and he was forced to fall back into a defensive position.

Paul spun. Now the guard's forearm was across his throat.

The guard chuckled, "You dumb shit."

Paul tried to respond, but the grip on his throat prevented the words from coming out and air from getting in. His head felt like it was going through the loop of a roller coaster. Light faded. His vision narrowed. He reached up and tried to punch the guard. The angle was wrong. The strikes were light slaps.

The guard laughed, "Good night, princess."

Paul's hands found the guards ears. He pulled.

The guard screamed and he twisted his head to lessen Paul's leverage. He pulled tighter against Paul's throat.

Paul pulled forward until the guard's chin was on top of his head. Paul let go of the ears, grabbed the guard by the back of neck and dropped.

The impact sent pain through Paul's tail bone and his head into the guard's chin.

The guard fell to the ground. Blood streamed from his mouth. Paul rolled onto his stomach and tried to regain his focus. The world blurred. He wheezed.

Brittany flailed at the second guard. An assault of limbs targeted his head and groin, each one deflected with a natural ease. His training was impossible for her to penetrate. He blocked kick after kick and an array of unpredictable punches.

However, his defensive stance did not block bullets.

Paul was beside her before the man dropped.

"You killed him."

"One shot, too. I'm getting better at this."

Paul grabbed two magazines from the fallen guard that matched the H&K in his hand. He fired several shots through the door to keep their pursuers behind cover.

They crossed the wide path in front of the casino, and tried to lose their pursuers in the maze of meandering walkways that ran across the island.

They took the path's tributaries without a destination in mind. Paul's legs ached; years of sitting on the couch had kept him free from gym-related injuries but did nothing to condition him for a wild weekend running gunfight. A half mile later a cramp had slowed him to a hobble.

"Run," Brittany said softly.

There had been no sign of their pursuers, but she was not about to stop running until they were safe.

"I can't run. I've never liked running."

"We don't have a lot of options," she said; she was wrong.

The path ended in front of a wide swatch of pavement that extended as far as they could see in both directions.

The test ring had been built on Master Key to fulfill the residents' love of expensive cars. Once operational, they would give driving lessons to the public for a price. A racing school was already in talks to open a branch of their school on the island.

They followed the track east for a tenth of a mile and found the answer to Paul Nelson's leg cramps. It wasn't pretty. It was yellow. A VW Beetle convertible sat poised on the racetrack ready to impress absolutely no one with its performance.

"What the hell?" Paul threw up his hands.

"They were doing a magazine shoot of convertibles."

"And this is what they brought? I'm canceling my subscription."

"It beats running."

"Not by much."

The keys were in the ignition. Paul dropped in behind the wheel.

"This is just going to take us in a circle," Brittany said as she climbed in beside him.

"We'll take it to the end and run from there."

He turned the key and the engine purred.

"Aww. What a cute sound." Paul punched the dash.

"I like it."

He put the Beetle in gear. Paul planned to drive in the dark. The car, however, decided it knew best, and washed the track with its halogens.

"Stupid car."

He mashed the gas and the Beetle responded – slowly. Drawn by the headlights, the guards scrambled onto the track.

Paul cranked the wheel and tried to run the group down. They scattered into the bushes as the Beetle hummed by onto the footpath.

"What happened to the plan with the track?" Brittany grasped the dash and dug in with her nails.

"It really wasn't much of a plan."

Paul fought the little car to keep it on the path. The twists and turns came suddenly, thrashing the pair about. The fact that he had not let off the accelerator made the turns that much quicker.

They found the main artery of the island and turned west. The path had been designed for foot traffic and electric carts, and afforded little in terms of width.

One of these carts soon crossed their path. Paul swerved to avoid it. Partially out of reflex, partially out of a fear of crippling the car.

They collided. Paul clipped the front wheel with his side of the car and turned the cart over. He chuckled.

A moment later they flew by another golf cart.

"If all we have to contend with is golf carts – I could get used to this car."

A jarring impact pulled them back into their seats and the roar of a powerful engine preceded another jolt from behind.

Paul adjusted the tiny rearview mirror. A convertible Camaro charged at them and mashed the rear end of the Beetle closer to the front.

"Hey, he didn't have to turn his lights on. And where did he get a Camaro?"

"From the shoot?"

"No fair, I didn't see that one."

"What difference does it make? Just outrun them."

"Outrun them?" Another crash forced Paul to make a dramatic steering correction. "That car is easily twice as powerful and, like, a thousand times cooler than this one. We're not outrunning anyone."

A fourth crash was quickly followed by a fifth.

"What do we do?"

Paul turned on the high beams and tried to read the road ahead. "We use this crappy car's crappy size."

He jerked the wheel violently and caught a side path. The Camaro followed.

Paul fought the wheel on the narrow cart path and somehow managed to toss Brittany the gun. It hit her lap and fell to the floor.

"Shoot!"

Every time she tried to grab the gun from the floor the violent shaking would drive her hands back to the dash.

Paul took another hard turn and found himself in the island's shopping district.

Designed like a mountain ski village, the paths did not get much wider. The buildings were set close to one another; small side streets branched off in every direction. The front wheel drive and lack of power allowed Paul to turn down the alleyways and drives without a squirrely back end. Paul had his edge.

The guard's heavy foot, combined with the power of the Camaro, caused the larger car to drift and crash into the walls of the boutiques that lined the path.

Paul stayed in the shopping center and worked his way in and around the square as he crossed and backtracked in the narrow confines. And, like a Tom and Jerry cartoon, the Camaro did its best to follow.

So far the guards had destroyed the Ralph Lauren, Coach and Sak's storefronts. Alarms rang out through the square as the cars raced around it.

A storefront window shattered as the Camaro's rear end swung wide and jumped the curb. It took out a support post, and the roof began to sag. The driver floored the Camaro to get clear of the falling debris, the wheels spun uselessly as white smoke poured from the tires. The roof collapsed and pinned the car beneath it.

Paul turned out of the square and headed north. The path narrowed again and they found themselves on the test track. He turned east and gunned the engine.

Brittany loosened her grip on the dash. Her fingers hurt from the tension and she found it painful to open them. She found the gun on the floor and handed it back to Paul.

"Hopefully, were done with this." He placed the gun between the seat and the console. "There's no way they're getting that Camaro out of there."

The silver Corvette traded paint with the yellow Bug as it slammed against them. The driver was alone and grit his teeth as he pulled away for another strike.

Paul cursed the Bug again and jerked the wheel to counter the Corvette's strike.

"Seriously? We got like the only crappy car they brought?"

The smell of burning rubber wafted past his nose, and the pull of the car momentarily decreased. The Corvette had rubbed the front wheel, slowing his progress.

The Corvette pulled away. Paul grabbed between the seats for the gun, but it was caught under the seatbelt latch. He was wrestling with the pistol as the Corvette collided with them again.

A fifth hit helped shake the pistol free; Paul aimed across his door and opened fire.

The Corvette's brakes chirped as the antilock brake system activated. The Beetle pulled ahead on the race track.

The Corvette rammed them from behind, trying to force the Beetle to turn toward the center of the track.

The first turn of the track was upon them. It banked steeply to allow maximum speed through the turn. Paul checked quickly to make sure Brittany was still buckled in. Out of sheer habit he had latched his own belt when he first got in the car.

They entered the turn.

"Just try and go limp."

Paul veered right. The Corvette went left. The little yellow convertible shot up the embankment and into the air as it cleared the lip of the track. The Corvette slammed on its brakes.

Brittany screamed. Paul squealed. The Beetle flew for only a moment before crashing into the beach. A wall of sand rose up around them as the car's body dug into the shoreline. The airbags deployed. The engine continued to purr.

Paul began breathing again and wrestled to get the car under control. It ran straight – no matter how much he turned the wheel, it ran straight. The impact with the surf was almost as rough as the landing. The car stopped instantly.

With the airbags already used up, Paul found nothing to stop his face from striking the steering wheel. His chin bled profusely and he found no desire to talk. Crashing waves beat against his head. The surf sounded muffled.

Brittany had struck the dash and was dazed.

Paul undid his seatbelt and stood to see over the back of the car. He swayed uneasily. His footing was uncertain.

The Corvette had made its way off the track and was still coming for them. He couldn't find his gun.

The silver 'vette slid to a stop in the sand. The driver stepped out and leveled a submachine gun at Paul.

"Get out of the car!" Paul heard him yell this just before a red stitching of bullet holes appeared across his chest. Paul spun to see a man beside him holding an assault rifle; smoke rising from the barrel. Dazed, Paul turned back to the car. Another man was helping Brittany from the car.

Paul fell back into his seat and peered through the windshield at the black launch from the Rainbow Connection. He felt a hand on his shoulder. He turned and looked into the face of a thick and burly man.

The hand on his shoulder was huge. The forearms were like knotted rope. Hairy, knotted rope. "Mr. Nelson."

The words swam in his head, fighting to get upstream as everything poured from his consciousness.

"We got your distress call, Mr. Nelson. We're the cavalry."

Paul passed out.

27

The large black craft crashed into the side of the jet-boat. Fiberglass cracked and the smaller craft capsized. Steve hit the water; he didn't see where Katherine went.

For a moment he could not get his bearings – what was up, what was down. There was no light in the water until the shadow of the black craft passed overhead.

He kicked violently as he tore off the tuxedo jacket. It was pulling him down. His shoes were working against him, as well; the heavy Sketcher oxfords felt like lead on his feet.

He broke the surface and spun, looking for the girl. The engine of the black boat roared in his ear, first to one side, then from behind. He turned and found himself face-to-face with the hull of the craft, looking up into the barrels of two shotguns. The bores were dark and deep. The eyes of the guards were hardened and cold.

"Drop the gun Bennett."

The gun? He had already dropped it. It was on the bottom of the channel, somewhere near the tux jacket. He raised his hands slowly out of the water. One guard shouldered his weapon, and reached for Steve's hands.

Steve ran through his options. He could try to pull the guard in, letting the weight of his shoes drag them both to the bottom. He might be able to get away. But he realized that it wasn't just his shoes dragging him down. It was his legs. It was his body telling him to quit. He had nothing left, and a desperate attempt at escape would certainly get both him and Katherine killed. Where was she?

"Over there, I think she's unconscious," a voice from the boat said. A splash followed.

Steve held his hands higher and grasped those of the guard. They pulled him into the boat. Two guards kept their weapons on him. But he was done.

A few moments later they sat Katherine beside him. She was awake and sputtering. A trickle of blood ran down her face and collected on her wet evening gown.

"The old man wants to see you."

Steve sat back in the bench and put his arm around Katherine.

* * * * *

Savage was waiting for them back on the dock. His grin was menacing.

"I told you we just wanted to talk. But you had to keep shooting at me. Baxter wants you alive. So you'll be alive."

The blow came out of nowhere. Savage hit like an ogre. Steve felt his head try to spin off his neck. He did not feel his body hit the dock.

Katherine screamed and lunged at Savage. A guard held her back. Savage approached her.

"And you, Ms. Bernelli. Baxter wants to see you too. And unless your prince here makes the right call...it's not going to end well for you. I hope he was worth it."

He cracked Katherine with the same strike that took out Steve. She saw it coming and rolled with the punch. There was just enough time before the second swing, to spit blood into the face of Rick Savage.

28

Paul's mouth tasted like rust. He rubbed his jaw and winced at the pain caused by the contact.

He remembered trying to bite off a piece of the Beetle's steering wheel, but little else. He didn't know where he was, who had brought him here, or what he was wearing, but it itched.

He looked down at his chest. A multi-colored hemp shirt draped from his shoulders and continued down past his crotch. He wasn't sure what the pants were made of, but they weren't pretty either.

Across the room was an open door. Whoever had him, trusted him. He sat up in the bed and leaned forward to peer around the door's opening. Before he could move toward it, a man walked in.

"Good," he noted Paul's upright and conscious position. "How's the face?"

Paul tried to mutter "Gorgeous," but spit out a mouthful of gauze instead.

"You busted yourself up pretty bad on that steering wheel. Air bags don't work well if you try to use the same one twice."

He hadn't even felt the gauze. He probed his teeth with his tongue looking for gaps. There were none.

"You kept them all. Though there are a couple you'll want to have looked at when you get back to the mainland.'

"Where am I?" Paul spoke carefully for fear of losing a tooth.

"You're on a ship called the Rainbow Connection."

"The hippie's ship?" He stumbled over the "s's".

"Yeah, sure." The man chuckled.

"Who are you?"

"We're the good guys, Mr. Nelson." A large figure filled the doorway.

"Friends of the environment. I get it."

David Jefferson entered the room. He was dressed in a black outfit. The sleeves were rolled up to reveal the massive arms that had pulled Paul from the car.

"No, we're not protectors of the planet; just the country. I'm Special Agent Jefferson – Homeland Security."

Paul lifted his arms to study the hemp shirt. "Whatever you say."

"Sorry about the clothes. The undercover wear was all we had."

"Where's the girl? Where's Steve?"

"Ms. Daniels is resting. We don't know where your friend is."

"We have to go get him." Paul rose to his feet. He marveled at what good the rest had done him. Jefferson pushed him back onto the bed.

"Relax, Paul. May I call you Paul?"

"May I call you Susie?"

Jefferson stiffened. "All right, Mr. Nelson."

"I want to see a badge or an arm patch or whatever you guys use."

"You don't believe me?"

"You shot at us. You chased us down in a big black boat and shot another boat out from underneath us."

David was stern, "My men never fired on you."

"They fired on Steve and his date."

David saw the conviction in Paul's expression. "Do you think, Mr. Nelson, that there is a chance that in the great blue sea, there may be more than one black boat? They were Baxter's men. But I guess we did shoot the boat out from under you. Sorry. It was defensive fire."

"What the hell is Homeland Security doing here anyway?"

"We're looking for a bomb."

Paul felt the answer came a little too easy.

"What?"

"We think Baxter has it. And we think you and your friend can help us. Tell us what you know."

"You first." Paul scratched at the shirt.

David's eyes narrowed. Paul met his stare with a look of complete contempt. Jefferson relaxed his gaze.

"Like I said, we're looking for a bomb."

"What kind of bomb?"

"A Mark-15 bomb."

"I don't know what that is."

"It's an old bomb."

"Okay, how old is it?"

"More than fifty years old."

"Why do you think Baxter has it?"

"Baxter is dirty; he has been for a long time. We can't prove this, but his ties go deep into organized crime, the cartels and terror groups. He's kept himself clean by hiding behind an army of lawyers and false fronts.

"We suspect that he uses this island chain as his own little duty-free store for smuggling contraband in and out of the country. An item on the shelf is a hydrogen bomb."

"Nuclear bomb?"

"Hydrogen. An old hydrogen bomb that has been missing from the U.S. nuclear arsenal for decades."

"If you guys lost a bomb, there would have been a movie about it."

"In 1958 a B-47 from Homestead Air Force Base in Florida was on a practice run. During the flight it collided with a fighter. Certain of a crash, the pilot jettisoned his cargo – a Mark-15 hydrogen bomb. The plane crashed in Wassaw Sound off Tybee island in Georgia. The bomb was never found.

"Baxter is topping his islands with sand from the sound. We think he was looking for the bomb. We think he found it and is going to sell it to whichever angry man has the deepest pockets.

"We've searched almost every island in this ImagiNation of his and still haven't found it."

"Didn't you hear? It has a new name now."

Paul told Special Agent Jefferson about the party and Baxter's impassioned speech about the Liberated States of America.

"He's not selling anything but time shares, G-man. A paradise destination all his own, run how he sees fit. With his little laws and his own immigration standards."

David digested the information. Had his men spent a year sneaking about the archipelago looking for something that wasn't there to be found? Was the dredging in Wassaw a coincidence?

They had hauled the Geiger counter over every island and it had never registered above ambient radiation. Had it all been for nothing?

There had always been the frightening possibility someone had gotten to the bomb years ago. A search in 2004 had turned up nothing.

"Don't look so glum. You've got him on treason," said Paul. "If you've got a yardarm on this thing you can hang him from it."

David stood and headed for the door.

"What about Steve? We can't just leave him."

"Wait here, Mr. Nelson." Jefferson and the medic left the room. They left the door open. Paul wandered through it into the ship.

* * * * *

The dredge approached island 38 and began to rainbow its load from the ship's massive nozzles. The fountain of mud soiled the water around the uncompleted island and drifted with the current. No soil struck the island. Island 38 did not need another round of fill, only a coating of sea sand that would be provided by the Pacific dredge later in the week.

The dredge's hopper needed to be emptied, though, and if they spread the earth on the island they might have buried Savage's men who now worked the earth-moving machines to uncover a chamber in the center of the island.

* * * * *

Warren Baxter's office had changed since Katherine had seen it last. Her eye had always been drawn to the French doors that overlooked the paradise that he had built; now she could not help but look at the massive "Liberated States of America" map that dominated the wall.

Baxter had had it created in an old-world style. Written in script, as if Ponce de Leon had discovered the water park and five-star resorts on his explorations. In truth, it had been illustrated and art directed by the same undergraduate student that was responsible for most of the park maps. Many of the locations were out of place. It didn't seem to bother Baxter.

He drew on his cigar and surveyed his land as Katherine and Steve were brought in. Steve stood on unstable legs, and, after only a moment, drifted across the room to a couch. No one moved to stop him. He collapsed on the elegant sofa and bled on the upholstery.

Savage's blow had left a gash on his temple; Savage had left the gash unattended.

"Sorry about your sofa." Steve's voice was weak.

Baxter fumed momentarily but quickly regained his composure. He turned to Savage.

"Was this necessary?"

"He's alive." Savage took a seat across the room, relaxing, perhaps against his will. Steve could finally see his own wounds taking their toll on the hardened chief of security. He had come after them with such fury that Steve was pleased to see that the rough and tough mercenary was human after all.

"Steve, my boy. I'm sorry it came to this," Baxter said, offering him a drink.

Steve huffed.

"I never intended for any of this to happen. I want you to be a part of what we are creating here. As your father would have been."

Steve's stomach dropped. So it was true. His father had been involved with the plot.

"Let's leave daddy out of this, Mr. Baxter."

Warren dropped his head and nodded. "You're right. It must be so much for you to take in. But, think of it. Not only did you inherit one of the greatest fortunes in North America, you stand to inherit a nation. A new world."

"I don't want it. What makes you think that they'll let you secede anyway?"

Warren smiled and bared his teeth. "America has overthrown its weight in the world, Steve. They've overstepped their bounds to the point where college students travel under the maple leaf instead of the stars and stripes. The world hates America. And, rightfully so."

"The L.S.A. offers a paradise set apart from the country the world detests. We want no part of the stigma that the States have earned. We can be a beacon of peace. As a matter of fact, in six months time we will be hosting a world summit."

Steve smirked.

"We would bear no animosity to the U.S.A. We don't want to be Cuba. We would be a partner."

"You already run this by the president?"

"The president is a fool."

"You may still need his permission."

Baxter's smile faded. "The president is about to be too busy to care about little old us. It's not as if we're a threatening regime partnered with the great red evil. We pose no threat to the U.S. We just want a chance to make it on our own without the actions of our host nation holding us back. These islands are for the world. A gift from us. A place free of society's ills. A place where you can feel safe. There would be no chance of that if America's enemies were ours as well."

Steve sat upright. Baxter smiled too much; but, for the first time his smile seemed genuine. He glanced over at Savage. He was obviously weakened, but his eyes were still sharp.

"Why me?"

"I feel I owe it to your fa..."

Steve held up a hand.

"Of course. We'll call it a sense of debt, then. And, of course, as you say, our withdrawal would not be openly accepted all across the Potomac. I have no doubt that in time, after we've shown them our true intentions that we would be welcomed in as a trade partner with open arms."

"But, until that time we will still need trade. Your fath... your companies hold such sway over the Canadians that you could provide our burgeoning nation with the supplies it needs."

"You have a lot of faith in the Canadians. What makes you think they won't feel like the U.S.?"

Baxter's grin got larger, "Because Canadians are too nice."

"I don't know. I don't know many Canadians."

"You know Mr. Campbell. He has been a great friend to our country all along."

Steve was silent.

"And, he's a nice man."

Campbell was nice. Aside from initial disbelief, Steve never had any reason not to trust the Canadian attorney.

"I don't believe you."

"Steve. Our intentions are nothing but the best. We only want to offer the world a paradise. And a paradise can't exist with the threat of terrorism."

"You think Al Qaeda is going to come for your hammocks?"

"Terrorist attacks persist to haunt the nation. It is my belief that it will only escalate. And, with those who would visit here, it would provide too tempting a target for them."

"I always knew there was something wrong with you," Katherine had been quiet until now.

"Ms. Bernelli, please."

"All this time I've been singing the praises of ImagiNation to investors, to venture capitalists, even my own family. And behind it all was a madman's grab for power."

"I never meant to mislead you, my dear."

"No! Then why wasn't I selling stake in a new nation? Because, no one would have bit."

"You would be surprised, my dear."

Steve's eyes glazed over and he thumped back on the arm of the sofa.

"Steve? I need an answer."

There was no response. Baxter walked to the couch and placed his hand on Steve's arm.

"Don't you touch him!" Katherine slapped the older man's hand away.

Savage rose and crossed the room.

Katherine ignored him, and turned her attention to Steve.

"Steve. Steve." She patted his face. He breathed heavily but did not wake.

Baxter held up a hand to his Secretary of Defense. "Katherine."

She turned with hatred in her eyes.

"I've done what I can. When he awakes it will be in your best interest – and his – to convince him. I want him as a friend. I do not need him. And you are completely expendable." Baxter turned to Savage. "Get them a room."

Savage spoke into his radio and three guards entered the room and removed Steve and Katherine.

Savage leaned against the desk until Baxter snapped. "Where's the dredge?"

"Dumping now."

"Is it ready to go?"

"Almost. We had to wait. There's been some activity on the island. We think it was the hippies."

"Sink the boat."

"Not a good idea." Savage said. "It would be pretty obvious that it was intentional. And who was responsible."

"We have a right to protect ourselves and our patrons. Besides, in three days the officials will be too busy to even care."

"What if plans change?"

"Plans won't change. Will they Mr. Savage?"

Savage straightened and made his way to the door. "Of course not."

29

Paul made his way to the bridge. Jefferson was talking to one of his men as they pored over a map of the chain. Notes were scrawled on each island; numbers and notations made some of the smaller cays hard to see.

"We're missing something." Jefferson muttered.

"What about Steve?"

Jefferson didn't even look up. "There's nothing we can do right now."

"I'll admit the FBI isn't the best with hostage situations. But, you're the law. You have to do something."

Jefferson turned his attention from the map. "You can't even tell us where he is."

"Find him."

"How?"

"You've got to have a man on the inside.'"

Jefferson was silent.

"You've been on this for years. You couldn't even get a man on the inside?"

Jefferson erupted. He was short and stocky but incredibly quick. Before Paul could move he was pinned against the wall. The agent was inches from his face breathing hot spit onto his cheek.

"I had a man on the inside you little puke! And, he died helping your girlfriend escape. I've lost two men here, and I'm not willing to lose anymore for some spoiled rich kid who didn't have enough sense to know what he was getting into."

Paul flared and shoved Jefferson off. Jefferson seemed stunned that Paul could muster the strength. "And you wonder why Baxter wants to form his own country?"

Jefferson said nothing.

"Give me my gun back. I'm leaving."

David nodded. Two agents grabbed Paul from behind.

"You're going back to your room, Mr. Nelson."

"Please, Susie. Call me Paul."

* * * * *

It was dark out. This, despite the crystal blue water, made it difficult to see the approaching frogmen. There were five of them moving toward the boat. Each carried a satchel draped around his neck. Each satchel carried a charge that would crack the hull of the Rainbow Connection.

* * * * *

Paul was thrown into his room. He bounced off the wall and rushed back to the door, as it slammed shut. He immediately tried the handle, and found that it opened, but when he pushed on the door, it was shoved back closed from the other side. He looked again at the handle and could see no lock. He assumed that he would stay guarded. He ran to a porthole and pulled it open. His shoulders were too broad for it to be of any use.

He paced the room looking for anything to hit the guard with. There were some books, the mattress, and a pillow. Everything else was bolted down.

He had just finished unlacing his shoe when an explosion echoed throughout the boat. Shrieking metal reverberated throughout the hull. The horrendous noise was followed by several more explosions.

Paul was thrown off his feet and against the wall. The unlatched portal swung open and struck his head. He fell and landed on the mattress. He rolled to the corner of the bed as the ship began to list. He struggled to his feet, lurched across the room, and grabbed for the door.

It was stuck. As the ship rolled, he wasn't pushing the door open so much as he was pushing it up.

"Hey!" Panic filled his voice as he charged against the door. It would open a fraction, and fall back shut. "Hey! What was that?"

There was no answer. The ship rolled further. Paul placed his feet against the bunk and shoved against the door. It opened further this time. The guard outside was unconscious, collapsed against the door. Blood seeped from his head. Paul held the door open with his shoulder and tapped the agent on the head.

"Wake up! Get up! Get up!"

There was no response; only more bleeding. Paul shoved at the door again, but even extended to his full height, he was short of being able to force the guard off the door.

His feet were wet. Paul turned back to the room. The porthole was still open and the ocean was trying to share the room with him. He let the door slam shut above him, and dropped into the water to close the porthole. It stopped the water from entering, but he judged by the angle of the floor that the ship wasn't sinking just because he left a window open.

The mattress floated next to him, making it difficult to maneuver. Paul grabbed the gray-striped fabric, and began to roll the thin padding. It wasn't much, but the rolled bundle would give him an extra foot and a half of leverage.

He placed it on the edge of the bunk, stepped on top, and shoved the door again. The guard had not gotten any lighter, but the added height gave Paul enough room to force the door open far enough for the agent's body to slide off. He grabbed the doorframe and pulled himself up into the hallway.

The amount of blood was tremendous. It had spilled into the doorframe, and coated his hands as he dragged himself to stand. Paul checked the fallen agent for a pulse, and was almost surprised to find one.

He knew that head wounds bled a lot, but whatever had struck the guard had caused more than a scratch and a nap. Paul grabbed the guard by his collar and tried to lift him. He suddenly regretted shoving Jefferson. Had he not done that, they may have posted a smaller guard.

He strained against the guard's weight, but managed to lift the unconscious agent onto his shoulder.

The walk was difficult. Odd footing and the guard's bulk slowed him down. The stairway at the end of the hall stopped him. The staircase was at a twenty-degree angle to where it was supposed to be. Paul couldn't climb the stairs as they were, or even use the wall as a floor.

"Help!" He shouted beyond the doorway, suddenly worried about everyone else. Was Brittany okay? She was hot and he was concerned about her safety. "Help! Uh, man down, man down!"

He wasn't sure if it was the timing or his use of the talk of the trade but two agents appeared at the top of the stairwell and reached out for Paul and their fellow agent.

"Get him! I can make it."

At the sight of a fallen friend, the two agents turned their focus from Paul. They pulled at the injured agent's arms while Paul did his best to lift the man by his belt.

The fresh strength of the men made it easy work, and Paul soon clambered up the tilted stairs unencumbered.

The commotion on the deck forced Paul to yell.

"Where's the girl?"

The agent shrugged. "Everyone's getting on the boats."

Paul fought for balance as he crossed the deck of the ship with the two agents. The ship's captain was at the bow, calmly delivering orders. The boats were already in the water. Jefferson stood beside the captain.

"Get me a count!" He spotted the two agents, the unconscious guard and Paul approaching.

"That's everyone." The captain said.

Jefferson nodded, and ran to help with the fallen agent.

"Did Nelson do this?"

The agent carrying the guard welcomed the extra hands in carrying his friend, "Not sure."

"It was the explosion! He almost drowned me blocking the door." Paul said. "What happened?"

"They're sinking the Rainbow." Another explosion rocked the boat and threw the men off their feet.

"There's no telling how many charges are left. Get to the launch." Jefferson got back to his feet, forced an orange life vest over the head of the wounded guard, and activated a blinking light.

He chose one of the guards, "You jump with him. Keep his mouth above the water."

They jumped clear of the rail. It was only a moment before they were pulled from the water into the safety of the launch.

"Into the water, Mr. Nelson."

"Are you going after them?"

"I need to take care of my men first. We've radioed for help. The coast guard will be by...eventually."

Another blast shook the men from their feet. Paul collided with the burly Homeland Security agent and they collapsed to the ground. Jefferson was on his feet first, and hoisted Paul up by his hemp shirt.

"Into the water." The shove sent Paul reeling backwards over the rail. He hit the water head first and struggled to surface. He broke free in time to see Jefferson clear the rail and land a good distance from him.

Jefferson surfaced next to the launch, and pulled himself from the water. He looked around at his men in the boat. The girl was in the boat as well. "Did we get everyone? Is everyone okay?"

One of the men answered, "Tony and Rob pulled Gary out. He hit his head pretty bad, but they're looking at it."

Jefferson nodded and stretched. The last blast had tweaked his back. Paul crashing into him didn't help. He reached his hand around to massage a tender spot on his back. That's when he noticed the missing weapon.

He felt the empty shell of the holster and glanced around the floor of the boat. It wasn't there. "Has anyone seen my gun?"

The crew began to look about their feet. David stood and looked into the dark water. "Has anyone seen Nelson?"

The crew turned their attention from the boat to the water. Paul didn't have a vest or a beacon and they strained to see into the darkness.

"Oh, no. Is he okay?" Brittany was shaken from the sinking of the ship.

"Little bastard's fine." He hadn't even felt Paul take the gun off of him. The blast and tackle had taken care of that. Even when he threw him over the side, he had no idea that Paul was holding his .45.

"Find him. He wasn't wearing a vest." His team responded with flashlights and a spotlight mounted on the launch. It was still difficult to see.

* * * * *

Paul kicked toward the stern of the ship. The swim was difficult in the hemp shirt, but the numerous pockets in the cargo pants made it easy to carry Jefferson's gun.

The stern of the Rainbow Connection was all but resting on the bottom. When it finally did settle, the superstructure on the deck would be only a couple of feet underwater. He swam close to the ship for cover. If there was another charge it would be the end of him.

As he swam he peered into the water looking for whoever had caused the blasts. He had no doubt that they were a safe distance away when they went off, but he didn't like the thought of an invisible hand pulling him underwater to drown.

The deck was even with the surface of the water and Paul pulled himself back onto the ship. He ran as if every step had another explosion under it waiting to go off. Fires lit the way as he looked for a lifeboat, a dinghy, anything that would float. Then he spotted it. A rubber-hulled Zodiac floated just above the deck, fighting taught mooring lines to stay afloat.

Paul waded forward to free it. The lines were almost too tight to untie. But, after struggling for a few moments, the lines loosened and Paul pulled himself into the boat.

The engine started instantly. He pulled the .45 from the cargo pants and turned the boat to Master Key.

* * * * *

Jefferson heard the motor and pointed the spotlight in the direction of the sound. Paul waved, just before the Zodiac moved beyond the range of the light.

The pilot dropped the throttle and began to turn the boat to pursue Paul.

"Stop." Jefferson dropped back into his seat.

"Don't you want to go after him?"

"Unless you want us all to paddle, we're not going to catch him with this full boat. Rendezvous with the others. And someone give me a gun!"

30

They dropped Steve onto the hotel bed. He bounced. Katherine rushed to him, and put her hand on his face. Repeating his name softly, she kissed him gently on the forehead.

One of the guards left. The other took a seat in the room's overstuffed chair and he watched the scene without compassion. But he did watch. He kept a constant eye on the couple.

"Are you just going to the sit there?" Katherine yelled at the guard. She was panicked. Steve had been through a lot – there was no telling how many times he had been struck in the head in the last 24 hours.

"Yes. Unless you try something. Then I'm going to sit here, but I'll also shoot you."

She turned her attention back to Steve. The bleeding had mostly stopped; the crust of a scab was beginning to form. He breathed deeply. Soundly. She watched his chest rise and fall. When she looked back to his face, his eyes were open.

Katherine was relieved; she couldn't speak.

"Hi," he smiled.

She laughed out of relief.

"Where are we?" He sat up next to her, unsteady.

"Are you okay?"

"I don't know. I'm pretty dizzy." He placed his arm behind him to hold himself up.

The guard rose and crossed to the bed.

"Mr. Baxter would like his answer."

"Answer to what?"

"An answer to his question?"

Steve looked at Katherine. "What's he...?"

Katherine looked horrified. "Don't you remember?"

"What is everyone talking about?" Steve asked.

"Answer now!" The guard shouted and brought up the butt of his rifle to strike Steve.

Katherine screamed.

Steve's hand flew from beneath the pillow and struck the guard in the throat. The sudden gush of blood ran down Steve's hand. The guard fell on top of Steve, soaking the sheets red in seconds. Steve struggled to push the guard off him, and squirmed his way to the edge of the bed. He was covered in more blood than Katherine had ever seen, and yet the bed continued to soak it up.

"My god, how?"

Steve held up his hand. A shard of glass was gripped tightly in his palm.

"That phone was the one thing I let Paul talk me into buying. I really liked it. And they broke it."

She looked at him for a long moment. "You were faking."

"I was faking. But I also had my eyes closed. Where did they bring us?"

"Down one floor. We're on six."

Steve turned the guard over. He still clutched his throat, but he was all out of blood. The gash on his jugular caused Katherine to wince.

Steve disarmed the guard, checked the chamber, and moved toward the door.

* * * * *

They would come after him. He knew it. And in truth Paul wanted them to pursue. He would lead them right to Baxter and Savage. Savage would shoot at them; they would shoot back. The good guys always win. Done.

But he didn't want them to catch him too quickly, so Paul wound about the islands and tried to approach Master Key from another angle.

The Zodiac was fast. The massive outboard propelled the light craft to speeds that even he wasn't comfortable with. He eased up on the throttle, and went as fast as he felt he could see.

He focused on the water. There was nothing to see elsewhere. All the lights were out. He was pointed towards a faint glow in the distance that had to be Master Key. He and Steve had now toured the islands extensively, and he knew that nothing was lit up like the big island in the middle. It seemed closer than he thought it should be, but then again, the boat was fast.

He rounded the corner. The glow put the lights at least three islands away, giving him some time before he had to slow down. When he rounded the shore, he was blinded by the light directly in front of him.

It wasn't Master Key. It was the unfinished island Steve had told him about. Powerful work lights stood on tripods, washing the island in light. These and the lights from a dredging ship created the glow he had mistaken for Master Key.

He pulled back on the throttle in hopes of getting away unseen. He knew he had been spotted when men on the island began shooting at him.

The sudden force from gunning the throttle was unexpected and almost pulled him from the wheel. He shot past the men on the island and turned away into the open sea.

He thought he was clear when the arc of the spout of the dredge changed. Tons of dirt poured into the water behind him. The slurry pumped from the hopper as a weapon, trying to sink his tiny craft. He turned towards the ship, hoping that the nozzle would find it difficult to track him so close to the hull. This allowed the wall of mud to get closer to him; the turbulence turned up the sea and forced his boat to its side. He turned into the wake and managed to steady the craft.

He powered past the bow of the ship and turned down its length. The nozzle could not find him here. Gunfire rained down from the ship. He couldn't tell if any struck the boat.

The Zodiac was incredibly fast. The dredge ship's hull appeared seamless as he soared by, as much in the water as above it. The waves weren't great, but the speed of the small craft launched him up their walls with a rhythmic regularity.

He approached the stern quickly and was met by another burst of gunfire. A smaller boat from the island held three men and was coming right at him.

He passed the boat in an instant. Their combined speeds brought them together so quickly that the men in the boat couldn't put their barrels on Paul. Paul drew the .45 and fired a blind shot to keep their heads down.

One of Savage's men flew from the boat and struck his head on the hull of the ship. Paul didn't even acknowledge his good fortune. He looked to the open sea ahead of him and realized that it was no escape.

He circled the stern of the dredge and shot back up its starboard side. There was no fire from above. Paul could only guess that the superstructure of the ship prevented the gunmen on board from crossing the deck quickly.

He enjoyed the break for only a moment. A shot whistled by his head. More followed. The boat was behind him again. Muzzle flashes punctuated its location in the night.

Paul drifted right, away from the ship. He pushed forward on the throttle despite the fact that it was already running wide open. The men behind continued to run next to the dredge. They knew what he knew. The open sea was no place to run.

Paul pointed the nose of the craft out to sea and then cut back to his left. The bow of the dredge was already behind him. He cut the wheel till it stopped and dropped to his left to fight against the pull. The boat behind had gained; if he flipped his own boat now, it wasn't a matter of getting caught, it would be a matter of taking a boat to the head.

The pump crew saw the Zodiac and turned the spigot to intercept him. Paul shot between the fire hose of earth and rock and the bow of the ship. The Zodiac skipped dangerously close to the torrent and threatened to spill Paul from the boat. The v-shaped hull held the water; he released the wheel. The boat straightened in the water as he fought to stand back into the pilot's position.

He turned in time to see his pursuers emerge from behind the hull. Their speed carried them into a downpour of rock and silt. The boat did not come out the side of the man-made maelstrom.

The fountain was coming back towards him. The gunfire was still coming but it was growing small in the distance.

Paul smiled and relaxed. He'd spotted another glow in the distance. It had to be Master Key.

* * * * *

The guard outside the door heard the latch, the gunshot, and nothing else. Steve disarmed him and handed the gun to Katherine.

"You know how to..."

Katherine raked the slide and disengaged the safety.

"Okay then."

They moved down the hallway, letting the carpet mask their footsteps. It was plush and their escape made little noise. They reached the elevator and pressed the call button.

Their hurried pace was countered by the slowness of the car. Steve waited silently at first; his hurried breathing soon gave way to laughter. He looked at the gun in his hand, the beautiful girl next to him, and the gun in her hand. He laughed harder.

She smiled. "What?"

Steve laughed from nervousness, from the shock of just shooting a man and slitting the throat of another with the shard of a broken iPhone. He laughed at the absurdity of it all.

"What?"

"I told Paul this place sounded boring."

Katherine began to laugh as well.

"If you had put this in your brochure, I'm fairly certain I wouldn't have come."

It wasn't funny. It wasn't meant to be funny. But, it sent them both over the edge into hysterical laughter. Steve's eyes began to water. Katherine lost control of her breathing and began to laugh and gasp for breath at the same time. Steve doubled over and wheezed.

The elevator signaled its arrival and the doors slid open. Steve fired two rounds, and the guard inside dropped to the floor. The mad laughter ceased. They stepped into the car and pressed the button for the ground floor.

31

Paul eased up on the throttle. He thought he'd heard voices but the roar of the engine made it hard to be sure. The engine's RPMs slowed; he was certain he heard something.

He cut the engine.

"Nelson!" The maritime radio crackled from the Spartan console of the pilot's stand. Jefferson sounded mad. He may have been yelling for a while.

"Answer me you little prick."

Paul examined the CB style transceiver and thought better of answering. He reconsidered, it wasn't as if the agent could stop him now.

"What?" He shot into the microphone.

"Bring back my boat!"

"No. If you won't save my friend, I'm going to do it myself."

"You are jeopardizing my mission."

"Right, your antique bomb. Good luck with that."

"Nelson this is an open channel!"

Paul said nothing.

"Nelson, you will be placed under arrest for obstruction of justice."

"Fine. Come and get me." Paul slammed the transceiver back onto its hook. It missed the catch and fell to the deck. Paul gunned the throttle back to full and enjoyed the sound the engine made as it drowned out Jefferson's voice.

He shifted his feet and soon found the cable from the radio getting tangled around his ankles. He struggled to pull the receiver back up and place it on the cradle, but he couldn't reach it while steering. He cut the engine again. Jefferson was still talking.

" ... consider the destruction, the loss of life if the bomb goes off in the U.S. Consider the families. Consider..."

Paul pressed the button, "the little children. The cats and dogs that your imaginary bomb wouldn't kill."

"It's real, Paul."

"Even if it was real. Baxter isn't taking anything off of this island. He's only bringing crap here. Check the ships."

"We are checking the ships."

"And you haven't found anything. Right. Every ship comes here full and leaves here empty. Even the dredges."

There was silence on the other end of the radio. This time Paul did not enjoy it.

"You aren't checking the dredges are you?"

The answer was slow. "No."

"There's one there right now... at the unfinished island. It's dumping its dirt into the water. It's not covering the island."

"Bring me back my boat."

Paul considered this. He had to turn back. They would need the Zodiac. He hung his head at the thought of his friend.

"This boat won't help. The island is swarming with security. The men on the dredge are armed. You're going to need the Coast Guard or the Navy. I'm sure you've got their number."

He set the transceiver back in its cradle and brought the boat back to full speed. He wouldn't be long. He was confident that he could rescue Steve and his girl and bring the boat back to Jefferson.

"Get to Master Key. Storm the island. Rescue Steve. Rescue the girl. And hope that Homeland Security can stop a nuclear attack on the United States. Simple. As long as I don't run out of gas."

* * * * *

Savage scratched at the dressing on his shoulder. It was a rush job, but he wanted to be the one to pull the trigger when Bennett turned down Baxter's offer.

The radio on his belt burst with static, his communications officer's voice followed.

"Chief?"

He had to reach across his belt with his left arm to get the radio. It was awkward but he was beginning to feel the full pain of the gunshot.

"This is Savage."

"I intercepted a signal. The eco-ship crew is Homeland Security. They're looking for Tybee... I think they know where it is.

Savage cursed. He thought he'd considered everything this entire time. Homeland Security? How had they missed it? Sinking the ship wouldn't be enough.

"Send everyone. I want them all dead and buried on 38. Stuff them in the bunker and cover the bitch up. If they make contact with anyone, it's over and no one gets paid. Understand? Send everyone!"

"The loading crew?"

Savage kicked the ground. "No. Get the Tybee on the ship and get back to the Intracoastal. If we're lucky we can still deliver it."

"The Feds will be missed."

"They'll be forgotten when a bomb goes off in the White House's front yard."

He ran to the docks and joined two of his men as the radio barked his orders to the rest of his regiment. Minutes later, thirty guards piled into the security boats and left the floating dock undulating on their massive wake.

* * * * *

"I can't get through. Even the emergency signal is just giving off static."

Jefferson looked inward to the island chain.

"They know. They're jamming the signal."

"Master Key has a communications center."

"That's where the interference is coming from. Did you try the satellite phone?" Jefferson motioned for his radio man to put the set down.

"No luck. It was destroyed when the Rainbow sank."

Jefferson thought a moment. "Peterson?"

"Sir," a young agent answered from the back of the boat.

"I'm going to drop you and the girl on an island. You will lay low until help arrives."

"Yes, sir."

"Carlson. Send three men to Master Key and take the radio room. Have them call in the Coast Guard, Navy, DEA, anyone who has a ship in the area, and instruct them to intercept the dredge. Then have the men find Bennett and Baxter."

The orders were given. Brittany and the young guard were dropped on the closest island. Peterson was given a radio and instructions to periodically try the emergency channel.

Jefferson watched the two disappear in the distance. He felt the weight of the gun in his arms and gripped it tight. He wasn't sure any of his men would make it through the night.

* * * * *

Savage's armada arrived at the site of the sunken Rainbow Connection. Floodlights from the security ships bathed the area in light. There was no sign of the crew.

Savage directed the light on his ship across the deck and saw it devoid of lifeboats and the launch.

"Find them. Kill them."

His second-in-command pulled the radio mic from his shoulder and directed the brigade. The boats split up and began their search to the find the crew of the Rainbow Connection.

Within moments only Savage's boat sat above the wreck of the Homeland Security ship.

"Take me to the dredge."

* * * * *

The Zodiac plowed onto the beach. Paul had cut the engine only moments before reaching land and ran the boat up onto the white sand beach. He leapt from the boat and ran to the cover of a nearby cabana.

The island was quiet. He listened for the whir of the electric carts and heard nothing. There were no footsteps, no crackling radios.

He was certain that after the attack on the Rainbow Connection, the guards would be on high alert, but he could detect no signs of heightened security.

He ran from cover to cover, and peered around each corner before moving to the next. The wet hemp shirt rubbed his chest raw and he was sure that at least one of his nipples was bleeding.

He reached the casino in a matter of minutes and approached its entrance while staying concealed in the bushes that lined the walkway.

He crouched for several minutes, looking for any signs of activity. He saw none. He considered finding a back way in. The balcony they had used to escape was not an option.

It would take time to move around back, and the bottom of the ladder was still sealed. It had been too long already. There was no telling if Steve was still alive. Stalling would only make his death more of a certainty.

Paul eyed the front door, and steeled himself for a frontal assault. He growled inside, breathed deeply and charged from the bushes at full speed toward the front gates of his enemy's stronghold.

He tripped on the paved walkway and fell forward to the ground. The gun flew from his hand and slid across the hardened surface; he caught himself with his palms and a knee, skinning each in the process.

He inhaled sharply and fought the pain. "Ouch."

It took a moment to locate the black .45 on the black footpath. The checkered grip dug into his skinned palm.

He took several more deep breaths and slowly limped toward the front door.

He peered through the smoked glass. There was movement on the other side. A muzzled flash pierced the tinting and Paul stepped back and raised the gun.

He screamed as he returned fire.

Shots fired from both sides of the door quickly filled the tempered glass with holes and fractures that spread like spider webs across the surface. Paul emptied the gun as the fire ceased from the other side.

He held the gun firm, the slide locked back. He had to have hit the gunman. How could he have missed?

A moment was filled with the sound of cracking glass. Fractures grew and spread. The stillness ended when the glass door could no longer hold itself together. The pane shattered and crashed to the ground.

Paul had missed. The gunman stood on the other side of the door. He stood like Paul's reflection; an empty gun in his hand, still pointed at the door.

Steve lowered his weapon first.

"What did I tell you about pointing a gun at me?"

Paul lowered the gun. It was only through some miracle that the two friends had not killed each other.

Katherine stepped through the casino entrance, straightened her dress, and examined the damage. "You two are the strangest friends I have ever met."

Paul didn't smile when he saw Steve. He smirked.

"I stole a boat. It's just down the beach."

"Does the radio work on this one?"

"Too well. Oh, and Baxter, he's into bombs."

"What do you mean?"

"I mean chances are pretty good that on that island, where you two were making out, there is a fifty year old hydrogen bomb."

"You're not making any sense."

"My best guess is that Baxter is planning to smuggle a reconditioned hydrogen bomb into the United States on a dredge. Blow up a good chunk of some city. Then use the resulting chaos to secede from the union and form his own nation. Does that spell it out for you?"

"I guess that sums it up nicely – that's a lot to take in."

"How do you know all this?" Katherine asked.

"Oh, right. The hippies are Homeland Security."

The couple stared at him in silence as they tried to adjust to the new situation.

Katherine spoke first. "Great. All we need to do is get to their ship and we should finally be safe."

"Well... Savage sunk the ship."

"I didn't think we'd been gone that long." Steve looked back at the casino and up to Baxter's top floor. "It sounds like we're just as screwed as we were before all this."

"Don't fret, Steve. We've got a little rubber boat and a full tank of gas. We should be able to get at least halfway back to Key West before we'll need to paddle."

Steve resigned himself to the situation. "Where's the boat?"

Paul led the trio back to where he'd beached the Zodiac. He wondered if it was still there since, in his haste he had not moored, anchored, or even asked the craft to sit.

* * * * *

They wound their way through Master Key. The island was quiet. Steve noted that he hadn't seen another guest since the party. He began to wonder if they had left the island when the shooting started.

The hostages were another story – they were most likely still under watch. Steve speculated that they were insurance if the bomb plot did not succeed. There was no threat to Baxter; he could still hide behind a terrorist alibi. Provided he killed everyone who knew the truth.

The Zodiac was still on the beach, a solid ten feet above the waves. Paul must have been running the throttle wide open when he hit the shore.

What none of them expected to see was another Zodiac pulling up alongside.

Three of Jefferson's men leapt from the second craft and ran at the friends. Paul raised his gun. "You can't have the boat back."

The agents approaching Paul knocked the gun aside and rushed past.

"Hey," Steve said.

The three agents moved into the interior of the island.

"Let's go. Mine is the one on the right." Paul started toward the rubber boat.

Steve turned back toward the island.

"Come on, Steve." Paul had one foot in the Zodiac.

Steve turned to Katherine. "They must be going after Baxter."

"Let them."

"They may need help." Steve took a step to follow.

"Whoa!" Paul started to jump from the boat. His foot stuck on the gunwale, and he had to hop to maintain his balance. "Steve, stop. You are not a soldier. You are a trust fund baby. And, to tell you the truth, you're kind of a wimp. Let the feds handle Baxter. We'll handle the running away."

"I have no intention of getting into another gun fight. But we can tell them the layout of the hotel – where to find Baxter's office. We can help."

"But the boat. Just the three of us. C'mon Steve. Rub a dub dub."

"If they can stop Baxter, we have to help. If they can save the hostages..."

The three agents were nowhere to be seen. They moved fast. Steve and Katherine started running after the squad.

Paul swayed back and forth. "Argh, I'd better get my picture in the paper for this."

* * * * *

The last man on island 38 fired up the Caterpillar front-loader and dragged closed the lid of the lead-lined bunker that had concealed the Tybee bomb for the last several months. A solid thud was heard when it settled into place.

He removed the chains and placed them on top of the bunker. Moments later the Caterpillar covered the cache and chains. He left the machine sitting on top of the hatch, concealing it, as always.

The mercenary stepped from the machine into the wet topsoil of the unfinished island.

"How is it?"

The man was startled to find his commander standing before him. He looked terrible. Pale and weak, but his voice still boomed with authority.

"The detonation charge was a perfect fit. Baxter's connection really came through."

"He's nothing, if not well-connected. It seems everyone owes him a favor."

A short boat ride later, Savage stood at the bottom of a rope ladder that hung from the side of the dredge ship. He spoke to the men in the boat. "Join the search. Those feds can't leave the islands."

Savage scaled the ladder slowly. The hole in his arm was slowing him more than he wanted to admit. He was greeted by more of his men on the deck.

"Where is it?"

One of the officers pointed into the hopper. The Tybee bomb sat on the bottom. The old hydrogen weapon was coated with rust, which was to be expected considering it had sat beneath a Georgia bay for nearly fifty years.

The casing was well-built, and had been sealed well – it was the only portion of the weapon that had taken any of nature's toll.

Restoration of the bomb had been simple; it was the only part of the operation that had proceeded ahead of schedule.

Savage still marveled at the weapon. The casing looked like a large iron keg. Ribs lined the riveted shell giving it the appearance of an obsolete steam engine. It looked antiquated. It looked useless. But the material inside the bomb still had the potential to shatter a nation and forge a new one.

"Cover it."

The officer waved to the bridge and the deck top engines roared to life. Savage watched as the boom arms of the dredge moved into position.

Rick felt more than he heard the powerful suction cutter heads spin to life. They dipped beneath the water and, seconds later, sand and water began filling the cavernous hold.

Savage could no longer see the bomb as the slurry filled the hopper.

The boom rose and the crew prepared to get underway.

Savage grinned.

32

They caught up with the commandoes. Emboldened by the presence of the agents, Steve, Katherine, and Paul had run quickly and joined the team across from the casino.

Winded, but still standing, Steve explained the situation, "There are no guards. At least we haven't seen any since our escape."

The agent in charge gestured toward the shattered front door. "So who shot up the door?'

Steve and Paul pointed to each other.

"Baxter is on the top floor." Katherine said.

"We're not here for Baxter."

"But, this whole..."

"Our first priority is the dredge. I'm sure your friend told you all about it. He doesn't seem to be good with secrets."

Paul began to argue. Steve held him back.

"Then why are you here?"

"Ever since your idiot friend here blew our cover, someone has been jamming our equipment. We can't reach the Coast Guard. We can't reach the Navy."

Paul raised his voice and pointed out to sea. "But the bomb is on that dredge."

The agent pointed to Paul with his thumb, "Told you he was an idiot."

Paul bristled; Steve held him back. "Can my idiot friend and I help?"

"No. Your best hope would be to take Ginger and Gilligan here, get back to the boat and find a nice little island to hide on."

"That's it. I'm gonna give my foot a three-hour tour of your ass." Paul stood up and grabbed the agent by the collar.

The agent didn't seem to move but in a moment Paul was on the ground. Two others had him pinned.

"I know where the communications center is." Katherine blurted.

The agent in charge looked to Katherine. "How?"

"I work here. Well, worked here. I'm fairly certain I've been fired by now."

The agent turned and took in the size of the casino. The complex was massive. "Let him go."

Paul was released; Steve helped him to his feet. "'Three hour tour of your ass?' That was the lamest thing I've ever heard you say."

"You know that's not true."

Katherine led the group across the path and through the shattered doors of the casino. Other than the corpse of a security guard, there was no one inside. Katherine led them past the elevator bay and through a staff door.

The glitz and din of the casino gave way to cold, silent concrete. The hallway extended for a quarter of a mile – the length of the enormous building. At fifty- to seventy five-foot intervals, another hallway or storage room intersected it.

They continued past the first several tributaries. Each man moved silently. Steve marveled at their lack of sound. Each wore a vest that looked as if it was designed to rattle. Knives, guns, smoke flares, all hanging from designated clips and bouncing with each step; but neither the men nor the equipment made a sound.

Katherine turned down a hallway and pointed to a door. "It's the next one on the right. Down the hall."

"You stay here." The agent pointed to Steve and Katherine, but shoved Paul a little for emphasis. "I'd take your weapons from you but we don't know what could be coming down this hall. I don't want either of you to even draw unless absolutely necessary. Even then I'll be pressing charges. Understood?"

Steve nodded. Paul saluted.

"Let's clear the air gentlemen." The agent took point as the team gathered around the hallway. There was a flurry of hand signals and the group moved together.

An agent kicked in the door and an explosion ripped through the small hallway and into the larger corridor. Steve grabbed Katherine and pulled her to the ground shielding her from the blast. Paul jumped on Steve. Katherine gasped as the air was driven from her lungs.

The smell of cordite hung in the air. The three stood on wobbly legs – their equilibrium shaken by the blast. They could hear nothing at first. Steve yelled at Katherine to see if she was all right.

She was shaken, and temporarily deafened, but nodded that she was okay. Paul stumbled. He double-checked to make sure he had not been hit. His pants were hole-less; the explosion had just thrown off his balance.

They had to shout to hear themselves speak, but over the roar in their ears they heard the screams.

"Wait with her." Steve ran to the intersection of the hallway. It was horrific. Blood and body parts were everywhere. One agent was on his knees. Steve saw no cuts, scrapes or missing limbs. The rest were dead.

"Are you okay?"

There was no response. The agent rocked back and forth on his knees. He seemed unsure of what to do. His weapon was drawn but trained on nothing.

"Are you okay?" Was he yelling? He couldn't tell.

The agent finally saw Steve approaching. "All of them! All of them!"

Steve focused on the agent. He looked him in the eyes. Steve couldn't bear the site of the carnage.

"Are you okay?"

The agent looked at him puzzled. The question finally registered and the man began to feel himself for holes, cuts, or shrapnel. First a look of relief crossed his face, then one of guilt.

"I was shielded; hadn't cleared the wall."

Steve put a hand on his shoulder and was quiet for a moment. He looked into the agent's eyes again. "Is the radio working?"

It must have seemed a foreign language. The agent stared at him a moment, processing the question; his ears had to be ringing worse than Steve's. Then he reached for the radio on his shoulder, and spoke rapidly into the handset. He paused, and then spoke again.

"No. It must not have been coming from here."

Steve peered into the communications room. A smoking mass of copper wires and twisted metal was all that was left. There would be nothing in that room that still functioned. Steve's heart sank.

"We have to stop that ship!" Steve was firm with the agent. He hoped the tone would keep his mind and his eyes off of his fallen friends.

"There's no way. Even if we could find the signal, I can't take a fortified position by myself."

Steve pulled out his gun. The agent quickly dismissed it. "No. We have to find another way to stop that boat."

Paul stepped into the conversation. "Where's Jefferson?"

"He's going after the dredge."

"Is that possible?" Katherine asked.

"Probably not. Not without someone on board."

Steve thought for a moment. "Can you fly a helicopter?"

* * * * *

He had no real plan. Jefferson had gathered what fuel he could. If he couldn't board the ship he would have to keep up with it until the radio signal cleared up.

With a few deep breaths, they had been able to salvage scuba equipment from the ship. Even with this, he wasn't sure how the five of them were going to disable the dredge, board it, or save the country from Baxter's bomb. He was running out of time.

The lights of the ship came into view. It wouldn't be hard to overtake it, but as they neared, he realized it would be all but impossible to board it.

Rotors thundered and turned the water around the launch into mist. Surprised, Jefferson brought his gun to bear on the helicopter. The Homeland Security agent rocked the craft gently. Paul waved and pointed toward the ship. Jefferson lowered the gun and smiled.

The helicopter rose and roared toward the dredge. Jefferson poured on the throttle and followed. They had a chance.

* * * * *

"I'm going to drop you as close to the deck as I can. Don't land in the hopper or you'll drown." Burnett dipped the chopper lower.

"I can swim," said Paul.

"Not in that. It's worse than quicksand. Aim for the deck. As soon as you jump, I'm pulling up. Ms. Bernelli and I will head for the coast – broadcasting the entire way."

Steve nodded. The gun was heavy in his hand. They had been nothing but lucky this entire time. He had only fired in self-defense, and now he and his friend were about to storm a ship crawling with armed mercenaries.

Their luck couldn't hold. But they had to try. If they could just reach the ladder and roll it over the side, Jefferson and his team had a chance at stopping the dredge and the bomb from Tybee.

He turned to Paul. His friend eyed the dredge with determination.

"You okay?" Steve asked.

Paul nodded. "This is stupid. But if we pull this off, it is so going to get me laid."

Steve gripped his shoulder. "Good luck. And thanks for everything Paul."

Paul put his hand on Steve's back. "You've been a rich friend, Steve. But, I want to say one thing."

"What is it?"

"This time I get to kill Savage."

"Fair enough."

"Get ready to jump." The agent dropped the helicopter and aimed straight at the deck of the ship.

* * * * *

Savage watched the helicopter approach. It had never been Baxter's plan to join them; the helicopter's presence could only mean that the plan had changed. Maybe the old man was having second thoughts about detonating D.C.

It didn't matter to Savage as long as he got paid. Sure he would sleep a little better without the megadeaths on his hands, but he didn't sleep much as it was.

There was nowhere for the chopper to land. Baxter would have to step off onto the deck. He was lucky it was a calm night. But still, why would the man risk it?

His men waved the craft in.

* * * * *

"They're waving us in," Burnett shouted, following the directions of the crew onboard the dredge. "They must think we're someone else."

"Sure, why would anyone but Baxter be in Baxter's helicopter?" Steve stepped back from the door in hopes of keeping the surprise a secret.

"This might actually work." Paul said.

Steve felt a hand on his shoulder. He turned. Katherine had unbuckled the harness and leaned in to kiss him. "Don't die."

Steve kissed her back. "I want to take you on a vacation when we get back."

"No beaches."

"No. No beaches."

Burnett circled wide around the dredge. The engines had slowed and he matched the speed. "Get ready."

33

The guard waved the helicopter closer. He had never met Baxter; he had only heard the talk amongst the men. Creepy. Old. But he was the man with the money. Hundreds of millions. He wanted to make sure he made it on board safely.

Savage approached the helicopter. He shouted to be heard over the roar of the rotors. "What's he doing here?"

"Not sure sir. We're still jamming the radios."

Savage peered into the dark of the helicopter. He couldn't see anything through the sliding door. He caught the eye of another guard and waved him over.

"Be ready for anything."

The guards drew their weapons.

The helicopter door slid open, and two men opened fire.

The guard in front was struck in the chest and fell backwards. Savage grabbed him. He held the wounded man as a shield as he reached for his own gun.

The shots kept coming as the now-dead guard collapsed on top of Savage. He dropped the gun from his hand as he tried to break his fall. He hit the deck hard and struggled with his one good arm to push his way from under the guard.

A second guard collapsed next to him, dead.

* * * * *

Steve and Paul stopped firing and dropped to the deck. They had barely cleared the skids, when the helicopter began to climb and head toward shore.

Steve felt the drop in his injured leg, but managed to stay on his feet as he landed on top of the ship's bridge. Paul hit the floor next to him and lost his balance. He careened into Steve, pushing them both towards the edge of the three-story structure. They both collapsed inches from the edge.

"Get off me!"

Paul stood and grabbed Steve's hand. "I got one."

"Was it Savage?"

"I don't know. But I really hope so."

"I think I got mine. It happened pretty quick."

The return fire started. It was coming from the deck below. The pair scrambled low to the cover of a large piece of equipment.

"Jefferson should be here soon. Did you see any ladders? Ropes or anything?"

Paul shook his head.

"We've got to find a way to get him on the boat." Steve risked a glance around the edge of the pipe. A whistling trail of bullets filled the air. Ricochets filled the early morning light with sparks.

He turned to Paul, "At the bow of the ship. Do you see the ropes hanging from the booms?"

Paul risked a quick glance.

"Okay."

"If we can get the boom arms extended it might give Jefferson and his men a chance at getting on board." Steve looked again.

"Should we split up?"

"Didn't you learn anything from Scooby-Doo? You never split up." Paul pulled the mag from the USP that he had taken off one of the dead guards. It was full. He had a second magazine in his back pocket and Jefferson's .45 tucked in his waistband. "I'll go. Then you go. Me. You. Me. You. Me..."

"I get it!" Steve turned and fired several shots into the deck of the ship. Paul fell more than he ran down the steps of the bridge, and began to fire. Steve followed and they leap-frogged their way down to the deck.

They duplicated this maneuver three more times before they came back into view of the men on the deck. Machine guns chattered as they dove for cover.

They returned fire sporadically. It had little effect in keeping the gunfire at bay.

"This sucks!" Paul slammed the butt of the gun into the deck in frustration. A shot fired and struck the bulkhead next to Steve.

"Dammit, Paul!"

"Sorry. Hey," he pointed to where the bullet had struck. The door to the bridge was open. "The controls are probably in there."

"Go." Steve stood and emptied his gun. Paul dove through the open door.

The suppressing fire returned, and Steve found himself pinned behind a piece of the steel superstructure. He yelled to Paul. "Get the booms in the water."

"Here," Paul threw the USP and two magazines to his friend and drew the .45 from his waistband. The cargo shorts fell slack and he tightened the string that served as a belt. "Stupid hippie pants." He chambered a round in the .45 and stepped into the bridge.

* * * * *

Savage wrestled himself free from the dead weight of the guard on top of him, and found himself having a more difficult time moving to the bridge than he'd expected.

There was no way for the men on deck to know that only two intruders had jumped from the helicopter. He was as much of a target as Steve and Paul.

It had taken a moment to find his gun; the tear in his side protested as he bent over to reach it. A quick touch confirmed popped stitches. He pulled his fingers away; they were crimson.

He made his way slowly down the rear access ladder to the deck below. The troublesome pair had disappeared down the starboard staircase; the rear ladder gave him the distance he needed to come up on them from behind without being too much of a target himself.

He approached the corner of the superstructure and risked a glance around the side.

Bennett was crouched behind one of the many routing pipes. He was doing his best to return fire, but could only risk a few unaimed shots at a time.

Savage sensed a lull in the fire and dove to the ship's rail. He lay low and crawled quickly to Steve's position. Bennett was trying to clear a jam. Savage leapt.

* * * * *

An empty shell stood upright in the ejector of the USP. Steve's desperate shots had become more measured. The large pipe provided more than adequate cover, and he only fired to stall the approach of the men. This would give Paul time to deploy the booms. Now if only Jefferson would arrive.

He cleared the empty casing and pulled the slide back, planning to wait a beat before he fired again. Half a beat in, the gun was struck from his hand. He turned to catch Savage's gun across his face.

His eyes rolled and things blurred before him. He fought the urge to pass out.

He fell back into the line of fire. Sparks lit his face as the bullets bounced off of the diamond plate deck.

Steve rolled back to his place behind the pipe, and kicked at the gun in the security chief's hand.

It flew free. Steve struck again at the wounded Savage. Savage caught his kick and dragged him back behind the pipe. The blows were fierce. Steve covered his head and struck with his elbows when he had the chance. The strikes pounded his chest and shoulders. He couldn't tell if the restricted position was causing Savage to miss or if the man was trying to break him all over.

"You. Are. Going. To. Die." The words measured against each blow. Steve felt a rib crack. Breathing caused him pain.

The gunfire had stopped at the far end of the ship. Certain of a kill, the men arose from their cover.

Savage yelled, "He's mine."

Before he knew it, Steve was dragged to his feet and thrust against the wall. He felt the broken rib shift and cried out.

"Cease fire!"

The order was echoed across the deck from more than a dozen voices. Savage continued to beat Steve as he checked him for weapons, the crimson scar glowing as rage filled the mercenary and LSA Secretary of Defense. He threw Steve forward, tripping him at the same time.

Steve rolled, hoping to land on his good ribs. The jarring still brought pain.

"What are you doing here Bennett?" He kicked him in the stomach.

Steve gasped. The gasp brought more pain.

Savage lifted him by his hair. "Where's Nelson?"

* * * * *

The bridge was unguarded with the exception of one man and the new captain. The first had his back to the doorway. Paul fired. The guard fell. The captain reacted quickly to the report of the .45 and spun to face Paul, a gun in his hand.

They fired simultaneously. Their first reports sounded as one. The captain's shot grazed Paul's left temple. Paul fired three more rounds.

The captain slumped over the console, and Paul stormed into the bridge.

He looked desperately for a button labeled "boom controls" and soon realized that his vision was off. He blinked and felt his left eyelid stick for a moment. Blood filled his eye. He wiped at it and was relieved to find the eyeball still intact. He felt his head and found the bullet wound.

He tried to staunch the flow of blood with his fingers while he continued to look for the magic button, but it ran through his fingers, and clouded his vision again.

He almost tripped over the body of the first guard. His feet still twitched. Paul tore a sleeve from the guard's pale blue shirt, tied it over his wound and wiped the rest of the blood away. It seemed like it would hold.

Beyond the guard's body, he spotted a cockpit. This had to be it. Cockpits didn't belong in boats. He fell into the seat and noted the two joystick controls on the end of either arm of the chair. In front of him was a lit computer screen; beyond the windshield he had a clear view of the deck.

The firing had stopped. Not good. He leaned forward to search for Steve. He bumped one of the joysticks and the port side boom jerked.

Steve came into view with Savage right behind him. He grabbed the controls and thrust them both out. He had to hurry. He had to save Steve.

* * * * *

The launch roared into the wake of the dredge.

"Any ideas yet?" Jefferson wished for an answer.

He received none.

"Head up the side of this bitch. I'll shoot myself a ladder if I have to."

The dredge was huge, the largest cutter suction dredge that could fit in the Intracoastal Waterway. From a distance, it looked like a mass of pipes sitting on the water. The deck was flooded with work lights and the engine churned rhythmically.

The Homeland Security agent waved to the boat behind him, directing them to approach on the port side. He had no plan. He had no hope. But there had to be something they could do.

"Sir," the agent at the wheel pointed at the ship.

He saw it. The dredge arms began to stretch from both sides of the ship. The answer dangled under each arm – a series of evenly spaced ropes hanging just above the water.

"Get me to those ropes!"

* * * * *

Savage turned at the groaning sound of the boom arms. The massive pipes broke from their cradles and stretched over the passing ocean below.

Savage spied Paul through the glass. "What the hell is he doing up there?" One of his men raised his gun to fire.

Savage raised his hand to stop him, "We can't show up in port with bullet holes. Go and get him."

* * * * *

Paul scrambled over the seat back, kicking the port controller as he went.

The port boom dove into the Gulf of Mexico and Paul dropped to the floor as the ship reacted.

* * * * *

The sudden drag shook the ship. Savage fought for balance, but Steve had seen it coming. He worked with the roll of the ship and dove at Savage. His rib protested. He ignored it.

He caught the security chief off his guard and off-balance. The two fell to the diamond plate deck.

Steve held nothing back. He came down on the mercenary's back and jabbed his fists into kidneys. He found the back of the man's head and dragged it across the grated surface. He kneeled on fingers and threw elbows.

Savage wailed. His men were still gaining their footing and could not fire for risk of hitting the signature on their paycheck.

Savage's elbow caught Steve in the throat, and he fell back from the attack, choking. He struggled to his feet in time to be tackled by Savage.

Steve landed on his back and rolled the man under him. He couldn't free his arms to strike so he dug instead. His fingers worked deep into muscles and flesh. He pulled, he tore, he twisted.

Savage rolled and ended up on top. Steve was face down overlooking the hopper.

He stared into the frothing mixture of mud and water. The port side cutter had been engaged and water poured into the bin.

He remembered the pilot's warning, and fought to stay out of the hopper. He knew that the water, soil and rock would kill him, but the thought of landing on a rusty H-bomb scared him even more.

Savage shifted back and began to lift Steve's legs from the ground. Bennett struggled to grab the rail behind and above his head. His arms flailed. His broken rib fought every movement.

"Don't worry. We'll throw Nelson in with you."

Steve felt his weight shifting for the worse and looked ahead to his watery and really dirty demise.

The gunfire startled him. It must be Paul. Why else would they start shooting?

Jefferson and his men swarmed the deck screaming, "Homeland Security, drop your weapons!"

This warning came well after they had started shooting. Half of the mercenary force was caught dead on their feet. The other half returned fire and the boarding party was forced behind cover.

"Don't worry, rich boy. There's still time for us." Savage shoved at Steve's legs.

Steve's hand found the rail; he clamped on and stopped the forward momentum. He prayed for the gunfire to stop and for the Feds to pull him back from the brink, even though he knew Savage had a better chance of dumping him into the slurry below.

His hand ached but he held tight and began to turn to face his attacker.

Savage sneered. The crimson scar had never glowed brighter. Steve kicked. His kicks were weak; Savage held his grip.

Unexpectedly, his grip weakened. Savage jerked wildly as three shots found their way into his right side. He tumbled back, reeling from the impact of the .45 slugs. Steve grabbed the rail with his other hand and pulled himself back to the safety of the deck.

Savage twisted around to face his shooter. An empty Colt .45 struck him in the chest and bounced into the hopper. Steve followed Savage's stunned gaze, and saw Paul running full tilt with a red and blue bandana tied around his head.

Paul collided with Savage shoulder first, knocking the bleeding brute to the ground. Savage didn't get back up.

Paul grabbed Steve and pulled him to his feet. Bullets buzzed around them. This time it was fire from their would-be rescuers. Paul helped his friend across the catwalk over the hopper to relative safety of the port side. They moved to the front of the ship. It was as far from the gunfight as they could get.

"Are you okay?" Paul asked when they were positioned behind cover. He had to shout over the roar of the pumps.

Steve grimaced with every breath. Every movement aggravated the broken rib. He rested against the rail. He couldn't respond.

"You should have blocked or something."

Steve looked at his friend's head and wheezed, "You should have ducked."

Savage screamed behind them and clanged across the catwalk toward them. Paul turned to intercept him, but he was too slow.

Savage didn't stop. He drove all three of them over the rail of the ship. Paul caught the railing, and felt his shoulder muscle tear as his weight dropped against the hull.

Steve and Savage hit the water ahead of the boom. Paul screamed after his friend.

A large hand grasped his wrist. "Your other hand."

Paul hesitated.

"Nelson. Give me your hand!"

He complied. Special Agent Jefferson pulled him back on deck. Paul lurched forward and caught the rail of the hopper. The water inside the tank flowed red.

"Stop the pumps! Stop the pumps! Stop the pumps!" Paul shouted, collapsing to the ground.

An agent found the kill switch and the roar of the cutter suction arm whirred to a stop. Water stopped flowing into the hopper, but the surface glistened with blood of its victims.

* * * * *

Paul heard nothing. He stared at the diamond plate, mouth agape. He did nothing. Spit ran from his mouth. He couldn't think. He wasn't even sure if he was breathing.

He wanted to pound the floor. He wanted to kill Savage again and again. But he could only stare at the blood-and-mud infused deck of the dredge.

"We've taken the ship." The voice came from outside the ship. It was calm. A job well done. They had gotten their man.

David Jefferson placed his hand on Paul's shoulder. He didn't really feel it. The voice in his ear seemed distant. He didn't recognize it as the man who had just saved his life. It was quieter than it had ever been. Almost soothing. The gruff exterior of the Federal Agent was shattered by the graphic scene before them all.

"Nelson?"

Paul did not react.

"Nelson. He caught the rope. He made it." Paul snapped back to reality. He stood and turned to the rail. Below the ship was the other boat from the Rainbow Connection; on the floor of the small Zodiac was his friend. He looked like shit, but he was alive.

Paul continued to weep. But the tears streaming down his face didn't sting like they had a moment before.

34

Three weeks later it didn't hurt to breathe. But it still hurt to laugh, and Paul wasn't helping ease the pain. Steve sat across from his friend at a Blackjack table in the Aria casino.

Paul wore an eye patch over his left eye; his right arm was in a sling. The four of them sat around the table in the high limit area.

Katherine was up in chips. Brittany was holding her own, and Paul was pulling stacks of black markers from the pile in front of Steve.

"Maybe you should quit doubling down on everything."

"I have a system, and so far I haven't lost a dime."

"I'm down 10 grand."

"Well, apparently, your system sucks."

Steve laughed and grimaced.

"That rib still getting to you, wuss?"

"At least I escaped without a beauty mark."

Paul flipped up the eye patch and felt the scar next to his eye. He shrugged. "Chicks dig scars. Right?" He turned to Brittany. She was busy doing the math on a string of cards. She busted and ordered another drink.

"I think it's rugged." Katherine said.

"Don't encourage him. I still can't get him to take the stupid eye patch off."

"Careful, Steve. With you out of commission and her good taste, you may lose more than your money tonight."

Katherine smirked, "He is not out of commission."

"I'm glad to hear that, Ms. Bernelli. I'd hate for that suite upstairs to go to waste."

"Thirteen," the dealer laid a five on Paul's eight.

Paul flipped the eye patch back into place and slid the rest of his chips in front of the cards. "Double."

"Paul!"

"What? It's a good bet."

"Bust." The dealer removed the thousand dollar stack. Paul was out. Again.

Steve pushed a stack his way.

Paul pushed it back. "No, I'm done here. It's time for some table service. Let's hit the bar."

* * * * *

They settled into the bar's VIP section. The girls excused themselves and the two friends watched them walk away. Katherine glanced back at Steve. Brittany kept walking.

"Paul, how do you know she's not after money?"

"I don't have any money. It's your money, so I don't mind." Paul topped off his glass and sat back in the booth. "I got a call from David today."

"And?"

"They found Baxter. They said he spent less than an hour in custody. He's got an army of lawyers twice the size of the force he had on ImagiNation, and plausible deniability. He put so much distance between himself and Savage that none of the investors are losing any sleep."

"What about the rest of Savage's men?"

"Nothing. There wasn't a real name among the files. The few that were guarding the hostages are probably working for a dictator somewhere. I just want to know how they got off the islands. I thought we took the only helicopter."

"What about Campbell?"

"They're looking into him. So far it looks like Baxter was bluffing when he said he was involved."

Steve was quiet. "What did he say about revenge?"

"He said it was unlikely. Baxter's goal is to distance himself from us as much as possible. But, he did say to keep an eye out."

"I find myself looking over my shoulder quite a bit."

"Me too. Like those guys over there." Paul nodded to a table across the room. Steve followed the gesture.

"I doubt it's anything. But they ordered a two hundred dollar bottle of Scotch just to get in here and haven't touched a drop."

Steve noted the full bottle. The men were large and unexpressive. They surveyed the room but never looked at each other.

"How long have they been sitting there?"

"They came in right after us. And I swear I saw them in the casino."

"Do you think they're following us?"

"Yes." Paul leaned in close and whispered, "You're paying them to." He leaned back in his seat with a smile and somehow a full glass. He raised the glass to his friend. "I hereby tender my resignation as your Minister of Security. People don't like you, my friend. And I am tired of getting the crap kicked out me for standing up for you."

Steve raised his glass. "I accept your resignation, because you sucked at your job. What are you going to do now?"

"I've taken on a new role – one filled with delightful challenges that are more in line with my interests."

"That is?"

"Grand Poohbah of squandering your fortune."

The two friends clinked their glasses.

"Oh waitress! More booze!"

- THE END -

* * * *

Join Benjamin Wallace's Readers' Group
to get a free novel and learn about the latest releases
and giveaways. And, because it's cool.

Go to BenjaminWallaceBooks.com to sign up.

* * * *

OTHER WORKS BY THE AUTHOR

Post-Apocalyptic Nomadic Warriors:
A Duck & Cover Adventure

The post-apocalyptic world isn't that bad. Sure, there are mutants. But, for the people of New Hope, daily life isn't so much a struggle of finding food or medicine as it is trying to find a new shortstop for their kickball team.

This makes it difficult for a post-apocalyptic warrior to find work. Thankfully, an army full of killers is making its way to the peaceful town and plans to raze it to the ground. Only a fully trained post-apocalyptic-nomadic warrior can stop them.

Two have offered their services. One is invited to help. The other is sent to roam the wasteland. Did the townspeople make the right decision? Will they be saved? Did they find a shortstop? What's with all the bears?

Find out in *Post-Apocalyptic Nomadic Warriors*, a fast-paced action and adventure novel set in a horrific future that doesn't take itself too seriously.

And follow more Duck & Cover Adventures here:

Knights of the Apocalypse (A Duck & Cover Adventure Book 2)
Last Band of the Apocalypse: A Duck & Cover Adventurette
Prisoner's Dilemma: A Duck & Cover Adventurette
How to Host an Intervention: A Duck & Cover Prequel
Gone to the Dogs: A Duck & Cover Prequel

Horror in Honduras (The Bulletproof Adventures of Damian Stockwell)

Raised from birth to be a force for justice, Damian Stockwell has forever trained to combat the evils of the world. Blessed with the physique of a demigod and one of the world's foremost minds, he travels to globe on a quest to confront evil and punch it in the face. At his disposal is a vast fortune, an endless array of gadgets and loyal friends.

Now, one of those friends has gone missing in a Central American jungle and the only clue is the grotesque image of a demonic tribal mask.

Dam and his trusted valet Bertrand rush headlong into danger and go face-to-face with evil incarnate to save their missing friend and attempt to destroy the Horror in Honduras.

And follow more of Damian's adventures here:

Terrors of Tesla
The Mechanical Menace

Dads Versus Zombies

They couldn't handle the Tooth Fairy.
John, Chris and Erik are neighbors happily living out the American Dream in the quaint subdivision of The Creeks of Sage Valley Phase II.

There were no winners against Santa.
To date, their only real problems have been with one another, raising a family and the draconian rules of the HOA. Although, they may have blown them out of proportion.

Their fight against democracy could have gone better.
A failed run for the HOA presidency has forced them together to work out their differences. Which is the only reason they are together when the dead rise from their graves.

And now there is a zombie apocalypse.
Now these three average dads must reluctantly join together to survive the spreading apocalypse and reunite with their families. Personal fears, long buried secrets and their own personalities threaten to tear the group apart as they make their way across the zombie ridden landscape in Dads Versus Zombies—the natural continuation of the best-selling short story Dad Versus the Grocery Store.

Originally published as *Dumb White Husbands vs Zombies: The Zomnibus*, *Dads Versus Zombies* is the sequel to the *Dumb White Husband* series of short stories.

ABOUT THE AUTHOR

Benjamin Wallace lives in Texas where he complains about the heat. A lot.

Visit the author at benjaminwallacebooks.com.
Also, find him on twitter @BenMWallace or on facebook.

Or you can email him at: *contact@benjaminwallacebooks.com*

To learn about the latest releases and giveaways, join his Readers' Group at benjaminwallacebooks.com.

If you enjoyed *TORTUGAS RISING* please consider leaving a review. It would be very much appreciated and help more than you could know.

Thanks for reading, visiting, following and sharing.
-ben

58414240R00148

Made in the USA
Lexington, KY
10 December 2016